PROVE IT, JOSH

Prove It, Josh

JENNY WATSON

sononis
PRESS

WINLAW, BRITISH COLUMBIA

Copyright © 2013 by Jenny Watson

LIBRARY AND ARCHIVES CANADA CATALOGUING IN PUBLICATION

Watson, Jenny, 1970-, author

　　Prove It, Josh / Jenny Watson.

ISBN 978-1-55039-211-1 (pbk.)

　　I. Title.

PS8645.A864P76 2013　　　JC813'.6　　　C2013-901977-4

Sono Nis Press most gratefully acknowledges support for our publishing program provided by the Government of Canada through the Canada Book Fund and the Canada Council for the Arts, and by the Province of British Columbia through the British Columbia Arts.Council and the Book Publishing Tax Credit, Ministry of Provincial Revenue.

Edited by Barbara Pulling
Copy edited by Dawn Loewen
Proofread by Audrey McClellan
Cover and interior design by Frances Hunter
Cover image courtesy Cusp and Flirt/Masterfile

Published by
Sono Nis Press
Box 160
Winlaw, BC VOG 2J0
1-800-370-5228

books@sononis.com
www.sononis.com

Distributed in the U.S. by
Orca Book Publishers
Box 468
Custer, WA 98240-0468
1-800-210-5277

The Canada Council | Le Conseil des Arts
for the Arts | du Canada

Printed and bound in Canada by Houghton Boston Printing.

Printed on acid-free paper that is forest friendly (100% post-consumer recycled paper) and has been processed chlorine free.

For Patrick

CHAPTER 1

In Irons

Josh put his finger on the word and tried to sound it out. "D-d-d-d..."

"*Because*," the tutor prompted. "It starts with a *b*, not a *d*. Remember?"

Josh tried again. "Because..."

It was Friday afternoon, the first week of summer vacation, and Josh wished more than anything he was out sailing in his boat, *Nomad*. Instead, he was stuck at the Arbutus Bay Public Library with his new reading tutor. He'd promised Dad he'd give the new tutor a chance, but the tutor made him nervous, with his shaved head and row of earrings in one ear. Even though he was only seventeen, six years older than Josh, he reminded Josh of one of Mom's boyfriends.

Josh kicked his shoe against the chair and scowled at a kid making faces at him through the window.

Across the table from him, the tutor tilted his chair backward and sighed. "Didn't you practise with your dad?" ·

"I told you, I did!"

The tutor raised an eyebrow. "Well, let's start again from the top of the page."

Josh slogged through the words, one at a time. It was like wading through the mud in his rubber boots at low tide. With every step, the mud caked his boots more and more, making them heavier and heavier.

By the time he got to the bottom of the page, his eyes smarted from staring so hard at the words, his neck was stiff, and a headache had started to pound behind his left ear. He snapped the book shut and shoved it across the table. "I *hate* reading."

The tutor sighed again. "Look... reading isn't easy for anyone in the beginning. You just have to memorize the sight words—the words you can't sound out easily, like *because* and *the* and *could*. And be patient."

"Like I haven't heard that before," Josh muttered.

Since grade two, when he'd fallen behind his

classmates in reading, writing, and spelling, Mom had been paying private tutors to help him. There had been the girl with the thick glasses who'd stayed after school to help him with his homework. And the old lady who smelled like cigarettes, who came to their apartment every Wednesday evening with a bag full of word games. And so many others, he couldn't remember their names. They all said the same thing. "Be patient."

As the tutor droned on, Josh looked out the window, watching the awning on the bakery across the street flapping and a plastic bag whisking along the sidewalk. In a breeze like that, *Nomad* would be flying. He could almost taste the salt spray misting across the bow.

"Josh." The tutor rapped his knuckles on the table to get Josh's attention. "Listen. Learning to read is like walking in the woods. Sometimes you trip over the roots. But if you watch where you're going and learn to step over the roots, you won't fall down. Do you like to hike?"

Josh shook his head. He hated hiking. One of Mom's boyfriends had taken him and his brother, Matt, one time, and they'd ended up bitten from head to toe by blackflies.

Exasperated, the tutor snapped, "Well, what *do* you like to do?"

Josh kicked the table leg, hard enough to hurt his big toe.

"Well?"

"I guess...I like...sailing," Josh said. And then he realized it was a trap. The tutor was going to say—

"Reading is just like sailing."

Josh smacked the palm of his hand against his forehead. "Yeah, right."

"I'm serious. What's the first thing you learned about sailing?"

Reluctantly, Josh thought for a moment. "You can't always sail straight where you're headed?"

"Right! You have to learn to tack."

Josh knew all about tacking—sailing in a zigzag pattern so that the sail could catch the wind. If you sailed straight into the wind, the sail just flapped and the boat sat still in the water. They called that being in irons. "So I'm in irons?" he asked slyly.

The tutor rolled his eyes. "Very funny. All I meant was that there are lots of things to learn in sailing, but once you know what you're doing, you can go places. And it's the same with reading. When you can read, books will take you places."

"Uh-huh." The only place books were taking him was the library, and that was the last place he wanted to be when the weather was perfect for sailing. Josh stole a look at his watch. Just ten more minutes. When he glanced up, the tutor was frowning at him.

"All right. You can go. But don't forget to practise over the weekend."

Josh nodded, but with his fingers crossed behind his back. There was no way he was going to waste the weekend reading when he could be out in *Nomad*.

CHAPTER 2

Boats, Big and Small

Outside the library, Josh tugged on his backpack, grabbed his bike, and pedalled down the hill toward the bay. Just past the ferry terminal, he took the gravel path that led to the marina where the *Jeanette* was moored.

The *Jeanette* was a thirty-foot cruising yacht, built for crossing oceans. She was a double-ender with teak decks, lifelines, and a traditional Bermuda rig, and much bigger than his boat, *Nomad*, which was just a dinghy. Dad had sailed the *Jeanette* all through the Gulf Islands, and once he'd even cruised as far as Hawaii. Now she was their floating home. But Dad had promised Josh that if he worked hard with the new reading tutor, the two of them, and Matt too, could go cruising for a week at the end of summer.

Matt was fourteen and lived with Mom in the apartment in Toronto. Josh had tried to convince Dad that Matt should come out to the West Coast to Vancouver Island to live on the *Jeanette* too, but Dad said Mom had made up her mind that Matt was going to finish school in Toronto. And when she made up her mind, there was no changing it.

Josh crossed the wharf toward the floating docks.

Mike, the marina manager, waved at him from his office doorway. "Good breeze, eh?"

Josh waved back. He would have stopped to talk, but Mike could talk the hind leg off a donkey, as he liked to say, and today Josh was in a hurry to get out on the water.

He clambered aboard the *Jeanette* and tossed his bag into the cockpit.

Dad was sitting with his back against the mast, reading one of his *Wooden Boat* magazines and drinking a beer. He was wearing his work dungarees, the ones with the holes in the knees, but he'd rolled them up and taken his boots and socks off. His feet were so pale compared to his weathered face and arms, they looked as if they belonged to someone else.

Josh pulled his shoelaces undone and took his

sneakers off too. He sat down next to Dad and felt the warmth from the deck soaking into his feet.

"How was reading today?" Dad asked, his bushy eyebrows raised in a question mark.

Josh shrugged. "All right." He picked at the lace on one of his sneakers. The plastic cap had a crack in it and he worked at it with his thumbnail.

Dad leaned over and nudged him with his elbow. "Stick with it, kiddo. You'll get the hang of it."

Josh grimaced and quickly changed the subject. "Could we take *Nomad* out to Senanus Island before dinner? I'm not hungry yet."

"Not even for ice cream?"

Josh opened his mouth and then closed it. Of course, he was always hungry for ice cream, but he was itching to take *Nomad* out. "Could we have ice cream tomorrow instead?" he asked.

Dad pretended to think about it. "I guess that could be arranged, but I'd require payment up front. I lost a couple of clamps in the water today while I was working on *Desiree*. Think you could dive down and get them for me tomorrow?"

Josh pumped his fist. "Deal!" he said. "C'mon, let's go now."

While Dad put away his magazine, Josh found

14

their life jackets and windbreakers. It was a warm day, but it would be cooler on the water.

At the dinghy dock, *Nomad* was tied up with the other small boats. She bumped gently against the dock as the water rippled, her varnished tiller and transom gleaming in the late afternoon sun.

Josh went through his mental checklist, just as he did every time he took *Nomad* out. Dad insisted he carry a bag full of safety gear—flashlight, whistle, flares, knife, first aid kit, emergency rations, drinking water, dry clothing, and, most important of all, a bailer.

When Josh had checked everything was in its place, Dad untied them and pushed them away from the dock, and Josh headed *Nomad* out into the bay. The wind had dropped a bit, but there was still enough of a breeze to send them skimming through the waves.

With everything quiet, there was just the gentle slap of water on the hull, the screeching of a lone seagull, and the buzz of a rubber Zodiac zooming past them on its way to the inlet.

Josh took a deep breath, inhaling the smells of seawater and mud, a hint of pine from the trees that lined the shore, and just the slightest sourness from the mill across the bay. The last rays of the sun peeked over the trees, casting everything in a magical golden light. With the tiller under his hand, he felt himself start to relax.

In the bow, Dad looked as if he was asleep, with his eyes closed, feet propped on top of the daggerboard case, and hands clasped loosely over his stomach.

Josh sailed on, enjoying the sights and sounds of the bay and the feeling of the wind on the sail. And then, watching the waves from the wake of the Zodiac rolling toward them, he had an idea. He stifled a chuckle and steered into the wake.

At first, *Nomad* continued to glide through the waves rolling toward them. But as the waves got bigger, *Nomad* began to bob up and down in the rough water, until finally a few drops of water splashed across the bow.

Dad sat up with a jolt, his eyes startled open. "What's going on?" He brushed at the water that had sprayed across his pants and looked all around.

Josh pretended to concentrate on something in the water, but he felt the corners of his mouth tugging up.

"You twerp! After a prank like that, I think it might be your turn to cook dinner."

Josh smirked. Reheating the leftover chili wasn't exactly hard.

Just then something warm and wet splattered in his hair. He wiped at it with a finger and screwed up his nose at the fishy smell. Seagull poop. "Ewww!"

Snorting, Dad pulled a rag out of his pocket and wiped at it. "You should have seen the look on your face! It's good luck, you know."

Josh wasn't convinced, but as he turned *Nomad* toward home, he laughed along with Dad. He guessed it had looked pretty funny—and he *would* need some luck to find those clamps.

CHAPTER 3

The Poster

The next morning, wearing just his board shorts and goggles, Josh stood on the dock next to *Desiree*, the boat Dad was working on. The sun sparkled on the water, but the cool breeze made goosebumps stick up on his arms. Josh tucked his hands into his armpits.

"The two clamps fell in here," Dad said, pointing into the water at the stern of the boat. "If you can find them, there's five dollars in it for you."

"Five dollars and a triple-scoop ice cream?"

"A double scoop."

"A double scoop with chocolate sprinkles?"

"Deal." Dad chuckled. "I'll be up in the workshop. Come and find me when you're done."

Josh grinned. This was going to be the easiest five dollars he'd ever earned. He pulled his goggles on and stood at the edge of the dock, looking into the green water.

Bracing himself, he took a deep breath and dived in. As always, the shock of the cold water made him stifle a gasp. Even in the middle of summer, the water here felt like snowmelt.

He swam toward the bottom. Down, down, down.

All sorts of junk hid in the swirling silt: old shoes, a bicycle wheel, a paint can . . . but no clamps that he could see. Seaweed swayed with the tide, and fish darted away from him as he peered all around. Swimming along the bottom, he saw crabs and sea stars, but still no clamps.

He surfaced and took a breath before diving down again.

This time, he swam away from the dock, farther and farther, until he saw a glint of sunlight catching on something metal. There was the clamp with its red handle. As he tugged it out of the silt, he saw the second one lying a few feet away. He grabbed that too and then kicked to the surface. After dropping the clamps on the dock, he hoisted himself up and sat for a moment catching his breath.

When he'd dried off, he pulled on his sweatshirt and then ambled across the wharf toward the main shed. Tucked under his arm, the clamps clinked and clanked together.

He was just about to pull the shed door open when he saw Daniel and his younger brother Alex trotting down the steps with Nathan and Corey from school. They were all carrying life jackets and fishing poles.

Josh paused with his hand on the doorknob. When he'd first met Daniel at the marina, he'd thought they might be friends, since Daniel spent a lot of time hanging out on his dad's boat too. But at school, Daniel avoided him, as if Josh had a contagious disease or something. Daniel wasn't the only one, either.

Now, as Daniel walked past, he shot Josh a scornful look. "Did you sign up for the Superhero Camp next week?" he asked the others. "It's at the library. Everyone's going."

"Not yet," Nathan said. "But I asked Mom, and she said I could go."

"Yeah, I'm going," Corey said.

Alex tugged at Daniel's arm. "Can I go too?"

"No, you're too young."

"Can I go next year?" Alex asked.

"Maybe." Daniel shook Alex's hand off his arm.

Feeling a twinge of jealousy, Josh trailed along behind. He'd wanted to sign up for the Superhero Camp too. At the camp they were going to be drawing their own superhero comics. But Dad had said he couldn't because he'd made a deal with Mom about Josh having a reading tutor over the summer.

Josh stood watching the boys help Daniel's dad load shrimp pots into his runabout, laughing and joking together. As the engine rumbled to life, Daniel's dad gave Josh a quick salute, and then he turned the boat toward the bay and roared off, leaving Josh standing alone on the dock with the water churning beneath him.

He traipsed back across the wharf with the clamps, wishing the boys had invited him along. Some days he really missed his friends in Toronto, especially his best friend, Brandon. They used to hang out all the time, riding their skateboards and building huge forts in Brandon's backyard out of old pallets his dad had got from the warehouse where he worked.

Josh had tried to make friends here in Arbutus Bay, but the other kids in his class weren't very friendly, especially when they found out he couldn't read.

On the very first day in his new class here, Mrs. Finlay had called on him to read a passage out loud. He'd never had to do that in Toronto, because all the teachers there knew he couldn't. And they knew that Mom had hired a tutor to help him. But Mrs. Finlay had made him stand up at his desk and read a whole paragraph, and all the kids in his class had whispered and giggled as he stumbled over the words and Mrs. Finlay corrected him. *Dumb. Stupid. Idiot.* That's what they all thought of him. It made him want to kick something.

He gave himself a shake. If Brandon were here, he'd make some joke about Daniel's dad's cowboy hat. He laughed to himself. That hat sure did look ridiculous on a boat.

This time, when Josh crossed the wharf in front of the marina office, he noticed a poster pinned to the notice board. Usually he didn't pay much attention to the notice board. There were just handwritten notices about things for sale, like old canoes and used engines, and people advertising dog walking with their phone number on little flaps that you could pull off. But this poster was something different. It was on shiny paper, and right at the top there was an amazing sketch of a sailing boat that looked so real it might sail off the page—and it was a boat just like *Nomad*.

Josh looked around to make sure no one was watching, then stepped closer and moved his finger along the black letters below the picture.

R-A-C-E

A race! He moved his finger to the words on the next line. The letters wriggled and jumped, but he kept his finger still and concentrated really hard.

Senanus Island Small Boat Race

August 24, 2 p.m.

Crews of 2

Under 15 years old

Prizes galore

Josh stumbled over the last word, but the meaning was clear: a sailing race with prizes!

Back in Toronto, he and Matt had entered a few races together at summer sailing camps. It had been fun sailing together and competing with the other kids. Maybe this race was a way he could prove to the kids here that he was good at something, and maybe he'd even make some new friends. And Matt would be here, so they could sail in *Nomad* together.

Excited, Josh headed back to the main shed and pulled open the door.

CHAPTER 4

A Double Scoop

Inside, Josh paused to let his eyes adjust to the dim light. One end of the shed was open to the outside, so even with the lights on, it always seemed dark inside.

An old fishing boat sat above the ways, propped up with jack stands and surrounded by a criss-cross scaffolding of planks. The ways, or marine railway, was a pair of short rails that sloped up a gentle ramp underwater, from the dock outside into the shed. The ways made it possible for Dad and the other workers to winch boats out of the water so they could replace through-hulls, zincs, and rotten planks without getting wet.

Josh walked across the uneven wooden floor. Splotches of glue and paint made shiny lumps underfoot, and he was careful to avoid a plank balanced in a precarious position. He didn't want to end up in the inky water that rippled below.

As he stepped around the end of the ways, a hideous wailing started up, so loud that he would have covered his ears if he hadn't still been holding the clamps. Jean, one of Dad's bosses, was perched on a plank. She had one steel-capped boot against the side of the boat for support and the other dangling over the water as she slid a power plane back and forth, firing wood chips in all directions. Wearing hearing protection and a face mask, she looked like some sort of alien. When she saw Josh, she pointed to the door that led through to the workshop.

Josh dashed the rest of the way, and when he entered the workshop he let the door thump closed behind him with relief. It was much quieter in there.

Dad was leaning over the workbench. The stack of plywood shapes in front of him, Josh could see, was held together with dozens of clamps and oozing glue. His dad gave the tub of epoxy another stir and wiped some along the next piece of plywood. "Hey, kiddo, give me a minute. I just need to finish this glue-up before the epoxy kicks."

Josh nodded. He knew that the glue hardened

really fast and that when Dad had mixed it up he had to use it quickly or throw it away. That was one of the cool things about Dad. He liked to explain everything he was doing. He treated Josh as though he was smart. Not like Mom, who was always in a hurry, coming and going from one important meeting to the next. She never explained anything.

Dad scraped a sticky layer of glue from the edge of a seam and wiped the waste on an old plastic lid. When he was finished, he rubbed his hands on his pants. "Phew. Glad that's done. I get nervous every time with all those little pieces and making sure there's enough glue on each one. But I see you found my clamps. Great!" He reached into his pocket and pulled out his wallet. "Here's your five dollars. Actually, it's time for a coffee break. Why don't we go get those ice creams now, eh?"

Together they headed up the steep, rickety steps past the blackberry brambles that reached out and grabbed at their clothes. They walked across the parking lot, and Dad led the way along the path that cut through from the marina to the corner store.

When they'd got their ice creams, both double scoops with chocolate sprinkles, they took them over to the park bench that looked out over the bay.

Josh licked at a dribble of ice cream that had crept down his hand. "So... did you see that poster on the notice board? The one for the race?"

Dad nodded. "Jean was telling me about it this morning. Are you going to sign up?"

"Yeah! It's when Matt's here, so I was thinking we could go in the race together. I'm going to email him when I go to the library on Monday."

"Sounds like fun." Dad crunched into his cone. "Mmm, chocolate is definitely the best."

"No it's not. Mint chip is better."

Dad laughed. "Remember that time we went out in Luke's boat on the lake and he'd forgotten the ice and we had to eat a whole tub of ice cream before it melted? You were still little then, just four or five years old."

"How could I forget? It was strawberry and I still can't eat that stuff. Even the smell of strawberries makes me want to puke."

"Those were some good days."

Josh nodded. That was before he'd started school, and before Mom and Dad had started arguing about everything all the time, and before Dad had quit his job and gone to school to learn to build wooden boats. They'd spent a whole summer staying at

27

Uncle Luke's cottage at Orillia on Lake Simcoe, and Dad had taught them all to sail. Even Mom had had fun, except when she fell overboard and Dad had to rescue her.

"Well, I'd better get back to work. What are you going to do for the rest of the morning?"

Josh shrugged. "I might take my sketchbook into the control room." The control room was a strange room in front of the marina office with windows that sloped outward. Josh liked to sit in there and imagine he was in a control tower, making sure the ferry and boats didn't run into each other. "I can copy the picture off the poster and send it to Matt." He found himself getting excited all over again at the thought of the race.

CHAPTER 5

The Bet

On Monday afternoon, after an overnight trip with Dad on the *Jeanette* to Sidney Spit, Josh was back at the Arbutus Bay Public Library for his reading lesson. It took forever and went no better than the last one, but finally he was free. He'd just passed the pillar near the information desk, on his way to the computers, when he heard the babble of kids' voices. One shrill voice was louder than the rest. Brittany!

"I'm going to enter the race," she was saying. "I got a new boat for my birthday. She's really fast. I'm going to call her *Hummingbird*. Hey, Amber, do you want to race with me?"

Josh groaned. Brittany hated him.

It was all because he'd laughed at her in class

for giving Mrs. Finlay the wrong answer about the St. Lawrence River. He hadn't meant to laugh. He'd just been so surprised she'd got it wrong, because he thought she knew everything. Since then, every chance she got, she had to prove how smart she was. And how stupid he was.

He quickly stepped behind the pillar and considered going back to the *Jeanette*. But he really wanted to email Matt about the race, so he peered around the pillar to see what was happening.

All the kids from the Superhero Camp were milling around. The camp had obviously just finished for the day.

Brittany stood by the library notice board with her friend Amber, as well as Daniel and some other kids from school. As usual, she was wearing all pink— a pink headband over her shoulder-length blonde hair, a pink T-shirt with a giant gold star on the front, a pink skirt, pink and gold sandals, and pink rubber bands on her braces.

Holding a pile of red and yellow flyers in one hand, she pointed, indicating Daniel should pin one to the board. "In the corner. That's right."

Josh looked from Brittany to the computers. Maybe he could sneak past and use the computer behind the reference desk. He tightened his grip on his backpack and sidled around the pillar.

"Hey, wharf rat!" Brittany screeched like a seagull.

Josh cringed.

"Shush!" reprimanded an old guy wearing a bike helmet and a reflective vest.

Josh inched forward, hoping Brittany would forget about him, but a hand clamped on his shoulder and spun him around to face the group. His bag fell to the floor, spilling out the book.

Brittany dropped the flyers and scooped the book up with sparkly fingernails. "What's this?" She looked at the cover with a smirk. "I read that in grade one," she scoffed. "Don't they teach kids to read in Ontario?"

The other kids snickered.

She opened the book and pretended to read like Josh, stabbing her finger at the page and sounding out the words.

"Give it back!" Josh snatched the book from her and stuffed it in his bag, his hands shaking.

"So J-Josh, did you see the poster for the boat race? Are you going to enter in your wooden bathtub?"

Josh hated the way she said his name, as if he

had a stutter, which he didn't. But calling his boat a bathtub, that was too much. He gritted his teeth. "Maybe."

"In that homemade thing? Don't be ridiculous!"

"*Nomad* isn't homemade!" Dad was a shipwright. Building boats wasn't something he did in his backyard for fun.

"A sail made from a blue tarp?" Brittany carried on. "That's so lame!"

Josh fumed. He felt like one of those cartoon characters with steam coming out the ears. He opened his mouth and the words tumbled out before he could stop them. "I bet *Nomad*'s faster than your boat. I bet I could beat you."

For a moment, there was silence.

Brittany raised her eyebrows and snorted.

Then all the kids started talking at once.

"Did he just make a bet against Brittany?"

"He's crazy!"

"He'll never beat her!"

Brittany put her hands on her hips. "Really?" she said. "You're so sure? Prove it!" She looked at the flyers lying at her feet.

Josh looked at the pile too, but he was too flustered to read the words.

"It's a bet!" Brittany continued. "When I win, you have to read at the library on Literacy Day." She pointed at the flyers. "See? I'm sure you can't read it, but it says the library's looking for volunteers to read aloud to the little kids. That's what you have to do if I win."

"No way!"

"Oh! Not so sure now, are you?"

A hush fell over the group as they all turned to watch him.

Josh clenched his hands into fists. No way was he going to read out loud at the library. He couldn't. His vision narrowed until all he could see was the pile of flyers on the carpet.

But what about those mean things she'd said about *Nomad*? *Nomad* wasn't a bathtub, and the blue tarp sail worked well enough. Someone had to stick up for Dad. And Matt would help him, wouldn't he? Maybe, together, they could win.

Josh took a deep breath and stood up straight. "Okay! It's a bet," he said, trying to sound tough. "But if I win the race, you have to do my chores at the marina. For a whole week."

"That will never happen," Brittany said smugly. At that moment, her phone rang. She held it up to

33

her ear, the pink and purple case sparkling under the fluorescent lights. "Yes, Dad?" She stuck her tongue out and looked at Amber cross-eyed.

Amber looked amused and shook her finger at Brittany in mock anger.

"I know... I'm coming." Brittany jabbed her finger at the Off button and pouted. She waved goodbye to Amber and the others, then curled her lip at Josh. "Stupid violin lessons," she muttered as she stalked off to the car waiting outside.

Josh dragged himself over to the computers. He pulled out a chair and sat down with a heavy sigh. Why hadn't he kept his mouth shut?

He logged in to his email. There was a new message from Matt. He double-clicked to open it, then grimaced as the words wriggled and jumped on the screen. He looked at them out of the corner of his eye until finally they sat still.

Whispering the words as he followed them with his finger, Josh read the message.

Hey Josh,

Mom signed me up for summer school so I can't visit until Christmas. Can you believe she forgot about our sailing trip?

Matt

Josh gasped. Oh, no! His chest tightened, as though two giant hands were squeezing the air out of him. Now what was he going to do? How could he win the race without Matt?

CHAPTER 6

Seahorses Café

Josh needed to call Matt right away. He wished for the millionth time that he had his cell phone, but Dad had taken it away.

"A cell phone's like a dog leash," Dad had said when Josh first arrived in Arbutus Bay. "You won't need one here."

Josh figured he had to be the only kid his age without a phone in the whole town. There was no phone on the *Jeanette*, either, even though they were moored at the dock. And no computer.

He logged off the library computer and dragged himself outside to the bike rack. As he unlocked his bike, Brittany's words played over and over in his head.

When I win... When I win... When I win...

Josh tugged on his helmet and told himself firmly to stop thinking about Brittany and her fancy boat. What he needed was a plan.

He coasted his bike down the hill to the ferry terminal and then turned onto the gravel path toward the marina. He pedalled as fast as he could. If Mike was still in the office, he'd call Matt from there. Maybe Matt could convince Mom to let him visit as they'd planned.

Josh didn't notice the old woman standing outside Seahorses Café until she was right in front of him. He jammed on the brakes and skidded to a stop, just in time.

The woman tottered backwards and put a hand out to the wall to steady herself. A few flakes of peeling paint drifted to the ground. "Careful," she said as she hitched her handbag strap back onto her shoulder.

"Sorry," Josh muttered. He flipped the pedal around with his toe. He should have been paying more attention, but he could hardly think straight.

"Makes you want to go sailing, doesn't it?" the woman said, pointing toward a copy of the race poster taped to the lamppost. She adjusted the glasses on her nose.

All the crazy thoughts in Josh's head slowed to a stop as he focused on the picture of the little boat. Absentmindedly, he let his bike fall to the ground so he could get a closer look. It was almost as if he were on the water now, feeling the sail fill with wind.

"My daughter-in-law drew that with charcoal pencils," she said. "Do you like it?"

Josh nodded. "It looks like my boat."

"You have a boat?"

Josh nodded again, all at once shy to be talking to a stranger. "My dad built her," he said. "She's called *Nomad*."

"Ahh," she said. "You must be Tom Parker's son."

Josh nodded, shuffling his feet in the gravel. Why was it always like this with adults? They knew you, but you had no idea who they were.

"Your dad built me a rowing skiff earlier in the year. Did a beautiful job too. He's a real craftsman."

Josh couldn't help but grin at that. He looked up and saw her smiling widely at him. He guessed he was forgiven for nearly riding into her.

"He told me you were coming out here from Toronto. How do you like it so far?"

"Okay, I guess. I like having my own boat."

"Well, Tom Parker's son, I think you should

have this poster, don't you?" She removed it from the lamppost and handed it to Josh. "I can replace it later."

Josh took the poster and touched the boat with the tip of his finger, almost expecting to feel the smooth wooden railing. But it was just paper. And a reminder of the bet. He ground his teeth.

"Is something the matter?" the woman asked. "Anything I can help with?"

Josh folded the poster into a neat square and tucked it in his back pocket. How could she help him? "No. Everything's fine. Thank you," he said.

She peered at him through her glasses. "Well, take care, Tom Parker's son."

Josh nodded.

When she'd gone, he unfolded the poster and read the words again. It clearly said *Crews of 2*, so he couldn't enter the race by himself. He refolded it and slid it back into his pocket.

Muttering to himself, he picked up his bike and pushed it the rest of the way to the marina.

CHAPTER 7

Bad News

When Josh got to the marina office, Mike was just locking up.

"Hey, Mike. I need to call Matt. Can I use the phone?"

In his black leather jacket and black jeans, and his motorcycle helmet under one arm, Mike was an imposing figure. But he was less imposing with his Boston terrier, Zippy, tucked under his other arm.

"Please! I really need to talk to Matt."

Mike looked at Zippy and said, "What do you think, Zip? Shall we give the kid a break?"

Zippy's tongue hung out of his mouth in a crooked grin, and he gave a short bark.

"The Zipster says it's all right, so I guess it's

your lucky day. But make it quick. I'm taking my lady friend out for dinner tonight, so I need to duck home and have a shower first."

Josh nodded and darted through the newly opened door. He punched the numbers into the phone and waited for Matt to pick up.

Except it wasn't Matt who answered, it was Mom.

"Hello?" Mom's clipped voice always cut straight to the point.

"Hi, Mom. It's me."

"Oh, how are you, darling? I haven't got much time. I've just called a cab to take me to the airport. How are things in Arbutus Bay? Did your father find you a new reading tutor?"

"Um, fine. Can I talk to Matt?"

Mom sighed crossly. "He's not home yet. So tell me, did your father find you a new tutor?"

"Yeah, he did." Josh picked at the corner of the table where the edge had come unglued. What could he say to convince Mom to let Matt come?

"Well, I've got to run. Glad you're doing okay out there." Josh heard her rustling through the kitchen drawer. "Good, here are my keys. I'll talk to you when I get back from this conference—"

"Mom, wait! I wanted to talk to you about—"

"There's the cab now. Got to run. Be good for your father."

Josh heard the line disconnect. Frowning, he put the phone down. She never listened. Some days he was really glad she'd given up on him and shipped him off to live with Dad.

Just as he turned away from the desk, the phone jangled loudly, making him jump. He checked the caller display and saw that it was their number in Toronto. "Can I get it?" he asked Mike. "It might be Matt."

"Okay, but make it snappy." Mike limped outside, favouring his bad knee, and lit a cigarette.

Josh swept up the phone. "Hello?"

"Josh? Dude, it's Matt." Matt paused to catch his breath. "I just got in the door and I heard Mom hang up on you, so I waited until she left and then I called you back."

Josh snickered.

"How are things with Dad?" Matt asked. "You're so lucky! I wish I was out there too. I checked on-line and it looks like there are loads of islands all around Arbutus Bay. Are you and Dad doing lots of sailing?"

Josh suddenly felt choked up. He really missed his

big brother. "How come you have to go to summer school?" he asked.

"Well, you know how I'm not that brilliant at math? Mom decided that if I took a math class over the summer, it might help me get better grades in the fall." Matt paused. "But guess what! I found out there's a robotics class, so I'm going to take that as well. Isn't that cool?"

Josh stared at the blinking light on the phone. He wanted to be happy for Matt, but all he could think about was the race and Brittany and how much he needed Matt right now.

"Josh? You okay?"

"There's this sailing race and I thought you would be here, so I agreed to this dumb bet and now I've got no one to sail with." Josh was close to tears, but there was no way he was going to let Matt hear him cry like a baby. "That's cool about the robotics class," he said, trying to be brave.

"Hey, dude. I'm really sorry. I was looking forward to hanging out with you and Dad, and a race would have been fun. Can you find someone else to go in the race with you?"

Josh shook his head, even though Matt couldn't see him. "I don't know. I don't think so. But it doesn't matter. Not really." That last part was a lie, of course. He sucked in a shaky breath. "I'd better go. Dad'll be wondering where I am. Thanks for calling back."

"Say hi to Dad."

"I will. Bye." Josh put the phone down and sighed.

Outside, Mike looked at him questioningly. "Everything all right?"

Josh shrugged. "Not really, but whatever."

Mike gently patted him on the arm. "That's no good. I gotta run now, but come and see me tomorrow. Maybe I can help."

Josh nodded. He couldn't see there was anything Mike could do, but it was nice of him to offer.

Down at the *Jeanette*, Dad was sitting on the deck with a magazine. "Hey, kiddo. I was wondering where you'd got to."

Josh sat down next to him, shoulders slumped.

"What's up? You look like you're not having a good day."

"I got an email from Matt. Mom signed him up for summer school, so he can't come until Christmas."

"Summer school?" Dad let out an exasperated sigh. "That mother of yours, she just doesn't get it. Kids need time to be kids. Summer's not the time for jamming in more schooling..." He launched into

44

his usual rant about Mom being a control freak and thinking that kids could be managed like a project.

Josh tuned him out. It wasn't that he didn't agree with Dad, but he didn't always want to hear it. Yeah, Mom could be difficult, but she was still his mother. And anyway, right now he had other things on his mind. "What am I going to do about the race?" he mumbled.

"What do you mean?"

"You know, the poster says *Crews of 2*, and I was going to get Matt to sail with me."

"Can't you ask one of the kids from school?"

"No!"

Dad raised his eyebrows. "Why not?"

"I just can't! Can't you call Mom and ask her to let Matt come?"

Dad shook his head. "You know that's not going to work. Once she's made up her mind, there's nothing I can do to change it."

Josh scowled at his shoelaces. The one he'd been picking at had started to fray. He scraped at the end until it split apart. Could his life get any worse? He thought about the seagull poop. It was going to take a lot more than luck to get himself out of this mess.

CHAPTER 8

A Distant White Sail

The next morning, Josh followed Dad up to the boatyard. The sun was shining and a steady breeze ruffled Josh's hair.

He dropped his backpack on the dock and sat at the picnic table outside the main shed. From there he could see the cars loading on the ferry. And just across the water, a few kids were fishing for crabs off the end of the pier outside Seahorses Café. He couldn't understand why they crabbed in the marina. The water was slick with oil and diesel and dotted with floating rubbish—plastic bottles, bags, and, worst of all for the seabirds, six-pack rings from cans of beer and pop.

Today the picnic table was a good spot for thinking. He pulled his pencils and his sketchbook out of his bag and opened it to a fresh page. He'd decided to make a list of all the kids he knew. But instead of a list of names, he'd draw cartoon characters.

He started with Brittany. He drew a circle for her face with round eyes and a little pointed nose, and then he added a wide mouth and braces across her teeth. Next he drew Amber with her long straight hair that was always perfectly parted in the middle. Then Daniel, with his ears sticking out a bit too far. Then Nathan, Corey, and all the other kids in his class. Each one was distinct.

When he was done, he drew a thick red *X* through the pictures of Brittany and all her friends, and then through all the kids who didn't sail, which was most of them. Being in the middle of farming country, the kids in his class tended to know more about horses than sailboats. That left just a handful of kids who he thought might be able to sail, and who were outside Brittany's club. But he didn't know anyone well enough to ask if they'd sail with him.

He flipped back to the drawing of the boat he'd copied from the poster. Looking at the picture brought back all Brittany's taunts. It made him want to crawl back into his bunk and pull the covers over his head. He *had* to find someone to sail in the race with him so he didn't have to read aloud at the library. He could see it now, the kids laughing at him and Brittany sniggering in her know-it-all way.

As Josh looked out over the bay, a couple of kayakers glided between the moored boats, their paddles dipping silently into the water in a comfortable rhythm. On the other side of the bay, a huge motor yacht with a helicopter on its deck swung on an anchor. Farther out, a small white sail zigzagged across the bay.

Josh slumped over the table. The more he thought about it, the more certain he was that he'd never be able to even enter the race, much less win it.

When Mike limped over from the marina office, Josh straightened.

Mike slid onto the bench across from him and propped his bad leg on the table's crossbar. "How's it going, kid? Did you find someone to sail in the race with you?" he asked. He sipped coffee from a huge travel mug.

Josh shook his head. Boy, news travelled fast through the marina. Sometimes, like today, it really bugged him. Couldn't anyone keep a secret?

Mike whistled tunelessly through his teeth, massaging his knee as he gazed around the marina, checking things out. When his eyes lit on the garbage bin, filled to the brim with pizza boxes and takeout wrappers, and surrounded by bottles and cans, he pursed his lips. "About time for a garbage run, isn't it, kid?"

One of Josh's chores was to empty the marina garbage bins into the dumpster at the top of the stairs.

"Yeah, I guess so," Josh said. He got to his feet and dragged himself over to the bin to sort it out. He held his breath as he pulled the bag out and tied a knot in the top. Even so, the stench of rotten food attacked his nose. As he hauled it up the stairs, he had a sudden vision of Brittany holding the leaky bag and getting smelly, runny goo on her sparkly sandals. The corners of his mouth tugged up at the thought.

When he'd finished, he went back to sit with Mike. Looking out at the water again, Josh saw the white sail far in the distance. "Who's that?" he asked.

Mike peered across the bay. "Oh, that's probably Dakota. She's a spunky wee thing. Lives in a floating home over at Anglers Marina."

"Spunky... ?" Josh asked.

"You know. Feisty, full of beans, sharp as a tack.

49

I hear she's been sailing since she was knee-high to a grasshopper."

They watched the boat with the white sail tack back and forth into the wind. Just then a loud roar broke the silence as a powerboat sped out of the inlet, leaving a giant wake behind it. The boat was headed right for Dakota.

Josh leapt to his feet, waving his arms and shouting. "Watch out!" But she was too far away to hear. He held his breath and crossed his fingers, waiting to see what she'd do.

Dakota's little boat seemed to hesitate for just a second before it swung around so that the bow faced into the wake. As the churning water rolled toward it, the boat crossed the wake straight on, bobbing up and down like a duck, but holding its course.

Josh let out his breath in a whoosh. She'd done exactly the right thing.

"Told you she was a good little sailor," Mike said, slapping Josh on the back. He called to his dog, who was scooting about, nose to the ground. "Come on, Zippy, let's get some lunch."

Josh's gaze drifted back to Dakota. How old was she? And would she sail with him in the race?

CHAPTER 9

First Mate

At Anglers Marina, Josh parked his bike in the rack outside the clubhouse and then wandered down to the dock to wait for Dakota. It was no wonder he hadn't been over here before. His heart was still pounding from biking up and over the ridge to the south end of the bay.

When Dakota sailed up to the dock, she threw him a line, which he looped around a cleat on the dock.

"Nice boat," he said, admiring the freshly painted hull.

"Thanks." Dakota stroked the railing. "She's all right." When she climbed onto the dock, the boat dipped in the water, as if nodding in agreement.

"So... ," Josh began. He jammed his hands into his pockets to keep them from shaking.

Dakota grinned. "So... sew your pants." She looked as if she was about his age, even though she was taller and skinnier than he was. A pair of glasses with blue plastic frames sat slightly askew on her nose. As she tugged off her hat, a lock of curly brown hair sprang out from behind her ear.

It reminded Josh of his mother's hair, which she was always trying to straighten with a flat iron or a new treatment at the salon. His own hair was a darker brown and wavy, more like Dad's.

"You're Josh, aren't you?" Dakota said, adjusting her glasses with a finger. "I've seen you around. Your dad works at the boatyard, doesn't he?"

Josh nodded. "How'd you know?"

Dakota shrugged. "My dad works part time as a carpenter. He did a renovation for the kayak rentals next door to the boatyard."

"Oh. So what about you? Mike at the marina told me you live in a floating home."

"Yes. The green one with the turret," Dakota said, pointing to one of the homes on the far side of the marina. "My bedroom's in the turret."

"No way!"

"Yeah, it's pretty cool. But you live on a yacht. That must be awesome. One day I'm going to live

52

on a boat." Dakota dragged her sail onto the dock and laid it out flat, ready to fold it up.

"Can I help?" Josh asked.

"For sure."

As they folded the sail together, Josh chewed his lip. He was having second thoughts. She probably wouldn't want to sail with him. This might be a giant waste of time. But the only way to find out was to ask her.

"So...," he started again. "Have you seen the poster for the race?"

"Of course!" said Dakota. "My mom did the drawing. She's an architect. And an artist."

"Are you going to enter?" Josh asked.

Dakota hesitated for a split second, then shook her head.

Josh raised his eyebrows. "Why not?"

"Well... I don't really know any kids here yet." Dakota looked away and went back to tying the straps around the sail. "We just moved here a few months before you did. We used to live in the city."

Josh felt his pulse racing. He dived in before he could chicken out. "Do you want to enter the race with me?" He paused, then rushed on. "My brother was supposed to be visiting, and I made a bet with this girl Brittany that I could win the race, but now I have no one to sail with." He stopped for a breath and rolled his eyes. "I don't know what I was thinking. There's no way I can win."

"I wouldn't be so sure," Dakota said. She looked back at her boat, her eyebrows drawn together. "But—"

"We can use my boat, *Nomad*," Josh said. "She has plenty of room for both of us."

Dakota nodded thoughtfully. "So what do you have to do if you lose the race?"

Josh grimaced. "Read at the library on Literacy Day."

"That doesn't sound so bad."

"Yeah, but I *hate* reading out loud."

"Well, what does she have to do if you win?"

"My chores at the marina for a whole week. What is this, twenty questions? Do you want to sail in the race with me or what?" He tried to sound like he didn't really care either way, but he tensed, hunching his shoulders and scuffing a shoe on the edge of the dock, waiting for her to say no.

"Sure." She said it so quietly and matter-of-factly that Josh thought he must be mistaken.

"You will? Really?"

Dakota nodded slowly. "On one condition."

"What sort of condition?"

Dakota crossed her arms, one eyebrow quirked up. "Give me a minute," she said. "I need to think of one." She rifled through her messenger bag and pulled out a chocolate bar. She broke off a piece and handed it to Josh.

It was Fruit & Nut, which he thought was a bit odd. Why not a Kit Kat or Reese's Peanut Butter Cup? He popped the chocolate into his mouth, wondering why things couldn't be easy for once. Who was this girl, making conditions, anyway? And why hadn't he seen her at school?

"How old are you?" he asked.

"Old enough!" said Dakota. "How old are you?"

"Eleven!" said Josh. "So?"

"Ten and a half!" said Dakota. "But I'm mature for my age."

"Yeah, right," Josh scoffed. "How come I haven't seen you at school?"

"I don't go to school," she said, looking pleased with herself. "Dad home-schools me."

Josh was puzzled. "If you don't go to school, what do you do?"

"Projects and other stuff," she said. "We have a

twelve-month pass for the Butchart Gardens, and sometimes we go to the aquarium in Vancouver, and we've been to all the museums in Victoria. You'd be surprised how many there are. At the moment I'm working on a project about migratory birds."

Josh couldn't imagine not going to school. No sitting in class, no math or spelling, no reading out loud. He'd never met anyone who didn't have to go to school. "Maybe your dad could home-school me?"

Dakota laughed. "I don't think so! Anyway, at least you get the summer off."

"Yeah... sort of," Josh mumbled.

Dakota slapped her knees in a drumroll. "The condition—I've got it!" she said. "I'll sail with you if you help me at Nan's."

"Okay," said Josh. "What do we have to do?" It was probably weeding or cleaning out the garden shed. Those were the things he helped his grandparents with in Toronto. It would be worth it if Dakota agreed to sail with him.

"Nothing exciting," Dakota said. "I promised Nan I'd help her sort through her newspaper clippings."

Josh's mouth was suddenly dry. He licked his lips. "What do you mean?"

"To put in her scrapbooks. She has one book

about the Olympics, one about gardening, and one about cooking."

Josh frowned. This did not sound like something he'd be good at.

Dakota continued. "When she cuts out the articles, she throws them in a shoebox. Once a year we have to sort them into piles so she can glue them into the right scrapbook."

"Well, um...," Josh stammered. "I don't know..."

"It's not that hard," Dakota said. "If you help me with Nan, I'll sail in the race with you."

Josh scowled. "Isn't there something else I could help you with?"

"No! That's the deal." Dakota stood with her feet apart and arms folded, the wind tugging at her hair.

"Look..." Josh paused, trying to think of some way, *any* way, to get out of it. "The thing is..." In his mind, Brittany mocked him. *Told you so*, he imagined her saying. *You'll never beat me in that homemade bathtub.* All at once it seemed like a no-brainer. He needed Dakota's help, and if that meant sorting newspaper clippings, that's what he'd have to do. "You win. I'll do it. Let's go and sign up for the race now."

CHAPTER 10

Making It Official

That afternoon, after Dakota got permission from her parents, she and Josh met at the marina office so they could sign up for the race.

"Got your entry fee?" Dakota asked, waving a ten-dollar bill.

Josh grinned nervously and pulled his money out of his pocket to show her.

Together they went into the office, where they found Mike slamming the drawer of the filing cabinet, a thunderous look on his face.

"What's up?" Josh asked.

"Thought I'd paid that power bill on time, and now they want to charge me interest because I was apparently two days late. Two days! What is the world coming to?" He massaged his temples with his fingertips and, taking a deep breath, sat back in his chair behind the desk. "Anyway, I see you two kids have met. That's a good thing. And I imagine you're here to sign up for the race, are you?"

"Yes!" Dakota beamed. She and Josh handed over their money, but Mike held up his hand.

"You can hold on to that until you've filled in your entry form." He handed them one from the pile on his desk. "Don't forget to get your parents to sign their consent at the bottom."

With the form in her hand, Dakota marched ahead of Josh out of the office. "We can sit at the picnic table and fill this out now," she said. "Or you could show me the boat you live on?"

"We can go back to the *Jeanette*, I guess," Josh said with a shrug. He felt a bit shy about it, because in the three months he'd been in Arbutus Bay, she was the first person he'd invited over. Well, really, she'd invited herself, but that wasn't the point. He led her along the dock, and when they got to the boat, Josh scooted up the steps and stepped aboard.

Dakota waited on the dock. "Permission to come aboard?" she asked.

Josh pretended to think about it and then said with a grin, "Welcome aboard."

Dakota slipped her shoes off and followed Josh onto the boat.

Inside the *Jeanette*, everything was varnished a pale gold. Red checked curtains matched the cushion covers, and a bronze lamp cast a warm glow over the cabin.

Josh shoved a pile of Dad's sailing magazines aside and showed Dakota his bunk with the storage underneath for his clothes. Above his bunk was a shelf for his sketchbooks, with a fiddle rail across the front to keep the books from falling off when the boat was sailing.

Dakota pointed at the books. "Can I see?" she asked.

Josh shrugged. "I suppose."

Kneeling on the bunk, she pulled one off the shelf and flipped through it. Her eyes widened. "These pictures are really good."

Josh squirmed. He didn't think the pictures were anything special. Drawing was just something he did when he was bored. To change the subject, he said, "Let's sort out this entry form."

"Here—why don't you fill it in while I'm looking through these," Dakota suggested, handing it over.

Reluctantly, Josh took the form. The tiny print

swam in front of him, taunting him. He'd never be able to concentrate enough to get the letters to sit still with Dakota watching. Biting his lip, he handed it back. "I bet you've got really neat writing," he said. "Why don't you do it?"

Dakota shrugged. "Not really, but sure." She quickly read through the form. "Name of boat, names and addresses of both crew, entry fee of twenty dollars, and parent or guardian signatures." She bent over the paper and filled in the information with small, precise letters.

While she did it, Josh shifted from one foot to the other, expecting at any minute that she'd thrust the form back at him and make him take over, which is exactly what she did when she got to the bottom of the page.

"Here, sign at the bottom," Dakota said, pushing the form toward him and giving him the pen.

Josh squinted. Near the bottom there were two spaces. He set the pen on the page in the lower of the two and started to draw a big *J*.

"No, no! That's where our parents sign." Dakota snatched the paper back and crossed it out. "You have to sign it here." She pointed at the space above.

"Oh, yeah, right," Josh said, grabbing the pen

61

back. He carefully drew the *J* again, and then *O, S, H*, and then *P, A, R, K, E, R*.

Dakota giggled when she took the paper back. "You wrote the J backwards," she said. "That's funny. My dad does that sometimes too." Josh stiffened, but Dakota sailed on. "So when should we go for our shakedown cruise? Can we go now?"

Josh shook his head. "I've got to do my chores." Actually what he had to do was meet his reading tutor at the library, but he wasn't about to tell Dakota that. "Tomorrow morning?"

"Are you sure we can't go now? I could help you with your chores."

Josh shook his head again.

Dakota shrugged. "All right, tomorrow, then." She bounded up the companionway stairs. "See you in the morning," she hollered as her feet hit the dock.

CHAPTER 11

Aye Aye, Captain

The next morning at ten o'clock sharp, Josh met Dakota at the dinghy dock. He'd left everything shipshape, the lines in neat coils and *Nomad*'s sail rolled in a tidy bundle.

"Sweet!" Dakota said. "Did your dad build her?"

Josh nodded, a swell of pride making him stand taller. "She's a Goat Island Skiff."

Nomad bumped against the dock gently as a wave rolled toward the beach. Her paint was thin in places, with scrapes and scratches where Josh had dropped his fishing rod, a reminder of the good times he and Dad had had together.

"So what's the plan?" Dakota asked. She dropped her messenger bag on the dock. It landed with a thud.

"What have you got in there?" Josh asked.

"Snacks!" Dakota said, and as if on cue, her stomach rumbled.

Josh rolled his eyes, but he did wonder if she had any more of the Fruit & Nut. "I thought we could sail out to Senanus Island to check out the course," he said. "C'mon, let's go!"

They put on their life jackets, and then Josh held the boat steady while Dakota climbed aboard. When she was sitting down, he untied the lines, pushed *Nomad* away from the dock, and, at the last minute, jumped aboard himself.

"Will you pull the sail up while I row us out?" Josh asked.

"Aye aye, Captain," said Dakota.

Josh grinned. Once they were clear of the dock, he shipped the oars and grabbed hold of the tiller. "Ready?"

"Ready!"

A light wind filled the sail, and Josh steered into the middle of the bay. The tiller trembled under his hand, as if *Nomad* were excited to be out on the water too.

"Will you keep a lookout?" Josh asked.

"Aye!" Dakota scrambled forward of the mast to

watch for rocks and crab traps. As they raced along, Josh saw she was beaming. "Isn't this great?" she said. "I can't imagine living anywhere else."

"Yeah, it's all right," Josh answered. It wasn't like sailing on the lake with Matt in Toronto, but Dakota was right. There was a lot to like here. He sat on the rail with his foot braced against one of the ribs, thinking about Matt. Was he stuck at home doing schoolwork, or was he out sailing too?

"Where did you live before this?" Dakota asked, as if she knew what he was thinking.

"Toronto."

"Is that where your mom lives? How come she doesn't live here too?"

"Mom and Dad got divorced a few years ago. My brother, Matt, lives in Toronto with her."

"So why did you move out here?"

"To get away from Mom," Josh joked, adjusting his grip on the tiller.

Really, it was too complicated to explain. The fights with Mom about homework, the yelling about his grades, and her weekly phone calls to Dad complaining about his lack of progress and inability to read. He guessed he would have given up on himself too, but it still stung that she'd shipped him off to live with Dad—and with only a few months left in the school year! It wasn't as if he wasn't trying at all in school. Reading just wasn't his thing. He pulled on the mainsheet and pointed *Nomad* closer to the wind. *Nomad* responded instantly, picking up speed.

Dakota threw up her arms and laughed out loud, and Josh realized he'd been holding his breath. He relaxed and breathed in the fresh air. Even though he was having a hard time with the kids at school, it wasn't all bad, living with Dad.

He and Dakota spent the next few hours sailing back and forth across the bay and eating Dakota's homemade granola bars. They practised tacking and jibing, and took turns at the tiller. On one tack, Dakota got her foot caught in a rope as she dived across the boat. And on a jibe, Josh bumped his head on the end of the boom as it swung across. But by the middle of the afternoon, Josh was more confident that they might make a good team.

Just as they were heading back, Brittany appeared from behind Senanus Island. In her new, super-lightweight racing dinghy, she skimmed the water, flying in the light breeze. She leaned out from the rail in her harness, hair fluttering, eyes hidden behind sunglasses. For a moment Josh pictured himself caught in a huge spiderweb with Brittany in the centre, bug eyes glittering at him as he tried to free himself from the sticky strands.

A spray of cold seawater across his face jolted him back to reality. Brittany was heading straight for them. And it didn't look as though she planned to give way.

"Captain... ," Dakota said.

"I see her," Josh growled as he veered away, pushing *Nomad* through the choppy waves to avoid a collision. As he watched Brittany, a lump caught in his throat, like a piece of the store-bought brownies Mom sometimes brought home for dessert, heavy and stale. Brittany's boat was fast. Much faster than *Nomad*.

Brittany crowed as she sped past them, "Told you, I'm going to win!"

"No, you're not!" Josh ground out. When he turned back to Dakota, she was looking all around, pretending not to see Brittany.

"Did you hear anything?" she asked, faking a bewildered look. She raised her eyebrows dramatically, then winked at Josh.

Josh smirked. "No, just the seagulls." But he was worried. How could *Nomad* ever beat Brittany's boat?

CHAPTER 12

The Discovery

Several days later, the morning dawned clear. But by ten o'clock, a heavy band of cloud had rolled in. Wind whipped the water into waves that slapped the dock and rocked the boats in the marina. Even though Josh usually loved the sounds out here, today the banging and clanking of the boats and the screeching of the seagulls set his teeth on edge.

He met Dakota outside the kayak rentals as usual.

"Rough, isn't it?" Dakota said, facing the bay.

"Too rough for sailing," Josh grumbled.

"How about we go to my place?" she said. "We could watch a movie. Mom found a copy of *Swallows and Amazons*."

"What's that?" Josh asked.

Dakota looked at him as if he were from another planet. "You haven't read *Swallows and Amazons*?"

Josh shook his head. "So? What's the big deal?"

"It's the best book ever!"

Josh shrugged. "Whatever."

"It's about four kids—John, Susan, Titty, and Roger—"

"Titty?" Josh snorted, but quickly covered it with a cough when Dakota glared at him.

"Do you want to watch it or not?" she asked.

Josh couldn't think of anything better to do. Anyway, he did want to see inside Dakota's turret. "Okay."

They biked over the ridge to Anglers Marina and left their bikes on the porch outside Dakota's house.

Josh followed Dakota inside.

"Mom!" Dakota yelled. "I've brought Josh back. We're going to watch a movie."

"All right," Dakota's mom yelled back. "You know where to find me."

"She's in the studio," said Dakota. "Come on." She led Josh upstairs. They climbed up and up, to the top of the house, to a blue door. Dakota threw the door open. "Ta-da! This is my room."

Josh stood in the doorway. The room was

octagonal, with eight narrow walls and windows all around. The wooden floorboards radiated out from the centre of the room, stained and varnished so that they almost glowed, like rays of sunshine. In one corner, Dakota's bed stood on stilts, with a desk and drawers underneath. Around the top of the room, so high up that you'd have to stand on a chair to reach it, was a long shelf strewn with giant shells, glass balls, and old boat stuff—a ship's bell, an old life vest, and a pair of binoculars. Lower down, there were other shelves filled with books of all shapes and sizes.

"Amazing, isn't it?" Dakota said, running a finger over the spines of all the books. "When I grow up, I'm going to be a writer. I read about this girl who lived in a turret, and she was a writer too."

Josh realized his mouth was open. He snapped it shut and stepped over to the windows. It wasn't so much all the books as the amazing view that had his attention. From the turret, he could see right across the marina. He could see the Arbutus Bay Lodge and Spa where Brittany lived, the ferry terminal, Seahorses Café, and the boatyard. He could even see as far as the *Jeanette*. No wonder Dakota knew everything that was going on.

Dakota scooted up the ladder to her bed and plucked the binoculars off the shelf. "Here, take a look through these," she said, offering them to Josh.

Holding the binoculars up to his eyes, he adjusted the dial so that the boatyard popped into focus. Dad and Mike were standing on the dock talking and gesturing toward Mike's wooden runabout.

He swung the binoculars back past the ferry terminal until he spotted something more interesting— Brittany washing her boat on the dock outside the lodge. He scratched at a mosquito bite on his chin as he watched her hose the salt water off the hull. He should scrub *Nomad* too. He hadn't cleaned the hull for days.

Dakota shifted impatiently. "Are you done?" she asked. "I thought we were going to watch the movie."

"Yeah, I'm done." Josh was about to put the binoculars down when he noticed Brittany leaning over the edge of the dock. Curious, he kept watching.

Brittany put down the hose and wandered along to the far end of the dock. She knelt down, looking into the water, then fished out a small crab. The crab scuttled away from her on the dock. She poked at it with her finger, lips moving, as if talking to it.

Josh's eyes watered from staring through the

binoculars. He blinked a couple of times to clear them.

Then Brittany's dad strode into view.

Brittany didn't seem to realize he was there until he was standing over her, pointing at the hose still gushing water beside the upturned boat. She leapt to her feet. Her arms flailed and her left foot caught against the edge of the dock. Then, almost in slow motion, she pitched backwards into the water.

Josh chuckled.

"What?" Dakota asked.

"Brittany fell off the dock." Josh kept the binoculars trained on her. When she surfaced, her face was the colour of a cooked lobster and she was spluttering.

Her dad stood with one hand on his hip, the other gesturing at the hose. He crossed his arms and tapped a foot while Brittany hauled herself onto the dock. He jerked his head at her, motioning in an angry way toward the hose again. Then he pulled his cell phone from his pocket, put it to his ear and walked away.

Brittany slouched over to the hose and turned it off. Then she grabbed her phone off the ledge by the boathouse and, shoulders slumped, sat on the edge of the dock, swiping at her eyes and texting. Probably telling Amber all about it, Josh thought.

Josh pulled the binoculars away from his face and turned away from the window. "Brittany's in trouble with her dad."

Dakota took the binoculars and climbed the ladder to put them back on the shelf. "He's always pestering her, especially now that her sister's away at music school. Dad says it's no wonder she's so insecure."

"You think Brittany's insecure?"

"Oh, for sure! Her sister plays the violin too, and she won a scholarship to go to school in the States. Dad found out all about it when he worked on their new kitchen. He says there's no way Brittany can ever measure up and that her parents' high expectations are just setting her up for failure."

"Her sister must be really good."

"She's always winning competitions, apparently."

Josh wondered what it would be like to have a sister who was brilliant. Mom was always comparing him to Matt, but it wasn't as if Matt was a genius or anything. He could read okay, and he got good marks at school, but he got into trouble sometimes too, like the time he'd got caught smoking behind the school gym. At least he wasn't perfect.

Josh almost felt sorry for Brittany. He wondered if she missed her sister the way he missed Matt. He watched her traipse along the dock, shoulders hunched and arms swinging stiffly.

But why was she so mean? Josh couldn't figure it out. She was even mean to her friends.

"Josh! Josh!" Dakota snapped her fingers at him. "Let's watch this movie."

"Yeah, yeah. Okay." He shoved Brittany out of his mind and followed Dakota downstairs.

In the den, they sat on the floor with their backs to the couch, watching the movie and eating more of Dakota's chocolate.

Josh couldn't believe what he'd been missing. Dakota was right. Only partway through the movie it was already his new favourite, even if it was a bit old-fashioned. He could see himself as John, captain of the *Swallow*, with his trusty crew. He tried to decide if Dakota was more like Susan or Titty. Definitely Titty, he thought. Titty was the imaginative one.

When the movie finished, Josh looked at Dakota, his eyes wide. "I wish we could have adventures like that. You know what would be really cool?"

"What?"

"If we camped on Senanus Island, like the Swallows camped on Wild Cat Island. We could even build a firepit so we could cook."

Dakota laughed. "We could, except that Senanus Island is an Indian Reserve. It's sacred ground, so we can't camp there. But if we sailed to the other side of the bay, we could camp at the provincial park near the ferry dock. I think they even have firepits there."

Josh mulled it over. "It wouldn't be quite the same as camping on our own island, but I guess it would do."

"I'll be right back." Dakota leapt to her feet and ran upstairs. A minute later, she was back. "You can read the book if you like," she said, thrusting a worn paperback copy of *Swallows and Amazons* into his hand.

"No! Um, thanks . . . no, really . . . oh, okay, thanks," Josh muttered. He took the book and tossed it into his backpack.

Dakota was nattering about the other books in the series and how she wanted to visit the Lake District in England, where the books were set.

Josh stood up. "I'd better get back to the *Jeanette* for lunch," he said. "See you tomorrow morning?"

"Of course!" Dakota said, bouncing toward the door. "Don't forget we're helping Nan with the clippings next week."

Josh stared at her. Goosebumps sprang up on his arms. He'd forgotten about the clippings.

CHAPTER 13

High Five

The following week, on Tuesday, Josh and Dakota biked to Dakota's nana's house on the outskirts of town. With a sick feeling, Josh followed Dakota through the front gate and along a gravel path that curved past a willow tree and round the side of the house. In the backyard, they leaned their bikes against the porch.

"Nan?" Dakota called.

Inside the house, a voice cackled, "Bedtime? Bedtime? Bedtime!"

A different voice answered, "No, it's not, you silly bird. You just had breakfast." An old lady opened the door a crack and poked her head out. A pair of pearl-rimmed glasses swung from a cord round her neck.

Josh's face stretched into a grin. It was the woman he'd met outside the café.

"There you are, dear," she said to Dakota. "I wondered what time you were coming. And I see you've brought a friend with you." She pushed the door open and stepped out onto the porch in her slippers.

Dakota kissed her on the cheek. "Hi, Nan. This is Josh. He's the one I told you about."

Dakota's nana looked over at Josh and winked. "Tom Parker's son. Good morning, young man. How nice to see you again."

"Bedtime, bedtime," the voice inside called again.

"Pay that bird no mind. It's as crazy as my husband was." Dakota's nana beckoned them inside.

Josh followed Dakota into the house. Inside, the kitchen was warm and friendly. Sunlight reached into the room through net curtains and reflected off the yellow walls.

Dakota's nana walked over to the counter and picked up a glass jug. "Iced tea?" she asked.

Josh looked at the brown liquid. Something was floating in it. "No, thank you, Mrs. . . . ." Josh hesitated.

"Mrs. Gordon," Dakota's nana said, passing him a glass anyway.

Josh took a sip. It tasted more like lemon than tea, and sweeter than he'd expected.

Dakota took a glass and gulped it down while Mrs. Gordon finished drying the dishes that were sitting on the draining rack.

"Brrring, brrring, Dolly, will you get that?" the bird called out.

Mrs. Gordon chortled. "What a crazy bird. That's what my Jack used to say every time the phone rang. Come with me, you two. Charlie obviously needs some fuss." She led Josh and Dakota down the hall. In the living room, by the front window, a huge blue parrot perched on a wooden frame made from arbutus branches.

"Hello, Charlie," Dakota said as she strolled over to the bird. The parrot stepped off his perch and onto her arm.

"Hello, hello, hello. Who's a pretty bird?" the bird asked.

Josh laughed, but he stayed by the door. Charlie's claws looked sharp enough to rip a hole in his sweatshirt, and his beak looked as if it could crack open an oyster. Not that Josh knew if parrots ate shellfish, but he tucked his hands in his pockets just in case.

While Dakota scratched the bird's chin, Josh glanced around the room. A grandfather clock stood in one corner, with a long pendulum ticking away the seconds, and an old globe, one of the ones you could spin with a finger, sat on a side table. Over the fireplace hung a huge painting of a sailing boat, and on the mantelpiece stood a handful of framed photos. Even from across the room, he could recognize Dakota in some of them. But it was something round and bronze that fascinated him.

"Is that a medal?" he asked.

Mrs. Gordon smiled. "Yes," she said. "I won that for sailing in the Olympics in Melbourne in 1956."

Josh gaped. "You were in the Olympics?"

Mrs. Gordon walked over to the mantel and traced the edge of the medal with her finger. "Yes," she said. "What a wonderful time that was. It seems like yesterday. I can still feel the calluses on my hands and hear the crowds cheering from the beach." She picked up a photo and smiled to herself for a moment before putting it back.

Josh was dying to hear all about it, but before he had time to ask, she'd moved over to where Dakota was standing with Charlie perched on her shoulder.

"Step up," she said to the bird, and he stepped

delicately onto her hand and then back onto his wooden frame. "Right. Let's get started on these clippings."

Josh felt the blood drain from his face. Why had he let Dakota talk him into this? "Um... I can't stay very long," he said.

Dakota shot him a look that said he'd better not even think about trying to get out of it.

"Well, it's very kind of you to offer to help," Mrs. Gordon said. "I'm sure it won't take us more than an hour or two."

Dakota pulled a shoebox out from under the couch and blew off the fine layer of dust that covered it.

Josh sneezed.

"Bless you!" Mrs. Gordon said. "Let me fetch a damp cloth for that. I guess the dust bunnies have been hiding under the couch again."

Picturing a row of bunnies huddled together under the couch, Josh felt his tension ease slightly.

Dakota wiped the lid with the cloth and upended the box on the coffee table. The clippings landed with a soft thump, some of them spilling onto the floor. "All we have to do," she said, "is sort these into three piles—Olympics, gardening, cooking. You can usually tell from the headline, but sometimes you have to read the first few paragraphs." She pointed out where each pile would go on the table.

Josh swallowed. *I think I can do this,* he tried to convince himself. *I can do this.*

He waited until Dakota and her nana had started, and then, hands shaking, he picked up an article. He took a deep breath and let it out slowly. He focused on the headline, but the letters shimmered. He waited and waited for them to sit still.

Sweet or tangy, cherries sure to please.

Josh breathed a sigh of relief. He recognized the word *cherries.* An article about food, so it must go in the cooking pile. Or was it about gardening? He looked at the photo and saw a picture of a pie. He placed the clipping in the cooking pile.

The next clipping didn't have a photo, so he quietly slid that one back into the pile and shuffled through until he found one with a photo of a sailing race. He waited until the letters on the paper settled down.

Olympic hopeful Richard Andrews wins big at Nationals.

Josh read slowly, one word at a time.

This weekend, talented junior Richard Andrews sailed to victory despite difficult conditions off English Bay in Vancouver, B.C.

The story was so interesting, Josh kept reading. He didn't notice that his finger was trailing along the paper or that he was mouthing the words as he tried to sound them out. Or that Mrs. Gordon was watching him from behind her reading glasses.

When he'd finished, he placed the clipping in the Olympics pile, wiped his sweaty hands on his pants, and reached for the next clipping. This one was about planting vegetables, so he put it in the gardening pile. The one after that was about baking ginger cookies. That one went in the cooking pile.

Sooner than he could believe, they'd separated the clippings into three piles.

Mrs. Gordon clapped her hands. "Well, that was quick," she said. "I think the third pair of eyes made all the difference."

Dakota beamed. "High five!" she said, holding up her hands so they could exchange high fives all round.

Relief surged through Josh. He'd done it.

CHAPTER 14

An Awesome Present

Back in the kitchen, Mrs. Gordon refilled their glasses with iced tea and joined Josh and Dakota at the table with a plate of peanut butter cookies.

Charlie perched on top of a giant cage. He stretched one leg backwards and, making mewing sounds, preened his chest feathers.

Mrs. Gordon broke off a piece of a cookie and passed it to Charlie. "So tell me about the course for the race," Mrs. Gordon said, passing the cookies to Josh.

"It goes around Senanus Island and back," Josh said, taking a cookie with one hand and reaching with his other for Mrs. Gordon's shopping list, which was sitting on the table. He sketched the course on the back. "It's a triangle. The start's by the inlet, the first buoy's northeast of the island, the second buoy's at the island, and then we finish back at the inlet." He bit into a cookie and made appreciative noises much like Charlie.

Mrs. Gordon sipped her tea. "What kind of boat are you sailing?" she asked.

"We're using my boat, *Nomad*," said Josh. "She's a Goat Island Skiff." His chest swelled with pride as he remembered the day Dad had given *Nomad* to him, not long after he'd arrived in Arbutus Bay. They'd launched her off the ramp at the boatyard and christened her with a bottle of ginger ale.

"That's a bonnie wee boat," Mrs. Gordon said.

"We're going to win the race," Dakota burst out. "Josh made a bet with Brittany."

"Dakota!" Josh scowled. It was one thing for the kids from school to know, but he didn't want the news getting back to Dad.

"Don't worry. Nan won't tell anyone, will you, Nan?" Dakota asked.

Mrs. Gordon winked. "Of course not! But that sounds like a lot of pressure to put on yourselves." She drank some more tea. "If there's one thing I learned from racing, it's to focus on things you can control, like how you trim the sails and how long you stay on each tack. Then you can be happy with yourself whatever the outcome."

Josh nodded. It made sense. But she didn't understand that he *had* to win the race or he'd have to read aloud at the library. And that wasn't an option.

"I've just had an idea," Mrs. Gordon said. "Wait here. I'll be back in a minute." She slipped out of the room.

Dakota walked over to Charlie and scratched his head. "Good bird, good bird," she cooed.

Charlie shook himself all over and nodded his head up and down and from side to side, like a bobblehead. "Happy bird, happy bird," he cackled.

Josh followed Dakota's example and rubbed the feathers on Charlie's head.

Charlie leaned his head to one side so that Josh could scratch around his ear.

"I can't believe you told your nana," Josh whispered. "I didn't want everyone to know."

"Don't be such a worrywart. We can trust Nan."

Josh wanted to trust her, but he wasn't sure he could. Like now, what was she up to?

"Here we go," Mrs. Gordon said, coming back into the kitchen. "Dakota, I've been planning to give this to you for a while, but now seems like the right time. Close your eyes and hold out your hand."

Dakota did as she was told.

Mrs. Gordon placed a round brass object in Dakota's hand.

Josh leaned closer so he could see.

"It's a compass," Mrs. Gordon said. "I had this in the pocket of my life jacket when I raced at the Olympics. It's my good luck charm."

"Wow! Thanks, Nan. It's beautiful." Dakota jumped up and kissed her nana on the cheek.

Mrs. Gordon turned to Josh. "Your turn, young man," she said. "Close your eyes."

Surprised, Josh closed his eyes. He felt something heavy placed in his hand. When he opened his eyes, he saw a leather pouch with a belt loop. He quickly opened the flap to see what was inside. It was a knife, but it was much better than the plastic-handled one in his emergency kit. This knife was a multi-tool with three blades of different sizes, a pair of pliers, a saw, and a screwdriver too.

"I didn't have that with me at the Olympics, but that Leatherman belonged to my husband."

Josh didn't know what to say. This was the best

present, other than *Nomad*, that anyone had ever given him. "This is so cool."

"Come here." Mrs. Gordon held out her arms.

A little embarrassed, Josh gave her a quick hug, noticing that she smelled like warm cookies. "Thank you!"

"Just remember, the most important thing is to do your best and have fun." Mrs. Gordon stood up. "Now skedaddle. There's still plenty of time for sailing this afternoon."

She walked them to the back door, whistling softly.

Dakota headed outside, but Mrs. Gordon snagged Josh's arm and kept him back. She spoke quietly. "Josh, I noticed you were having trouble reading the clippings."

Josh gulped.

"Don't worry about it," Mrs. Gordon said. "Nobody can be good at everything. When Dakota's dad was your age, he struggled with reading too. He had dyslexia." She wiped her hands on her apron. "I don't know if that's your problem, but I can help you if you like, the same as I helped Dakota's dad."

Josh stared at the floor. A crack in the linoleum ran from the doorway across to the kitchen counter.

He wished the crack would open up and swallow him whole. His ears burned. Had Dakota heard?

"You can think about it," Mrs. Gordon said. "But if you want some help, you know where to find me." She stood with her hand on the kitchen door, waiting for him.

In a turmoil, Josh sat down and slumped over the kitchen table, his head in his hands. His palms were sweaty and panic rose like a giant bubble in his chest.

Why was it always the same? Everyone bugging him about reading? Mom, Dad, his teachers, his tutors. And now Mrs. Gordon too. Except that Mrs. Gordon wasn't really bugging him. She'd offered to help, but she'd said it was up to him to decide. And she hadn't embarrassed him in front of Dakota. And she was a sailor. And she did make good cookies. And she'd given him the knife.

The kitchen clock ticked away the seconds while he tried to decide what to do. He went over to Charlie's cage, where the bird shuffled his feathers and stood on the edge of his perch with his head pressed against the bars.

Rubbing Charlie's head through the bars, Josh tried to picture himself sitting on his bunk in the

Jeanette with Dakota's book open in front of him, reading all the words without stumbling. A lump formed in his throat as he imagined Dad with a look of pride, seeing Josh read a real book like that.

"Okay," he whispered to himself. And then, before he could change his mind, he said it out loud, to Mrs. Gordon.

"Okay."

CHAPTER 15

Pirates and Purple Martins

Later that week, after Josh and Dakota had once again sailed to Senanus Island and back, they decided to sail up the inlet to practise tacking and jibing in a more confined space. The wide mouth of the inlet beckoned them, but the rocky, tree-lined shores soon narrowed so much that they had to turn every couple of minutes to avoid running aground.

By the time they'd sailed halfway up the inlet, Dakota was joking, "We could probably do this blindfolded."

"Ready about," Josh yelled one more time, before he leaned on the tiller and swung *Nomad*'s nose toward the other shore.

Dakota ducked and the boom swung across smoothly. The sail flapped once and then filled with wind, sending *Nomad* scooting forward. "Pretty good, but I bet I could do it better," she said.

Josh turned *Nomad* into the wind. "Let's swap. Your turn, smarty-pants." As they glided to a stop, he scrambled aside to let her take his position at the tiller.

As Dakota turned them back toward the other shore, a family of Canada geese, paddling in a line from biggest to smallest, split up and darted out of the way.

"And try not to run into anything," Josh said. "Like that branch!" He ducked as Dakota took them closer to an overhanging tree than he would have liked.

Dakota retorted, "I know what I'm doing." Then, as they slipped past the first of the boats moored in the inlet, she said, "Hey, check out that black sloop with the bowsprit. That looks like the kind of boat a pirate would sail, don't you think? Look, it's even flying a Jolly Roger!"

Sure enough, a small black flag with a skull and crossbones flew from one of the halyards.

"Why would a pirate be moored up here?" Josh asked. "I can't imagine there's any treasure."

"Maybe they've come to watch the fireworks. I'll

bet even pirates like a good fireworks show." She told him that, in the summer, the Butchart Gardens held concerts on the lawn and fireworks displays on Saturday nights. "If you're moored in just the right place, you can see the show for free between that gap in the trees."

Nomad bobbled as Dakota leaned to the left to show Josh the spot.

"Whoa, watch out," Josh said.

"We should bring *Nomad* up here one Saturday night. We'd just need to borrow some lights."

Josh nodded, excited at the thought.

"Hey, let's go all the way to the end of the inlet and see if there are any birds in the nesting boxes," Dakota said.

Josh nodded. "We might have to row. I think we're losing the wind." With the shores so close and the trees so tall, the water here was quite sheltered from the wind, making it a perfect spot for mooring, but not so good for sailing.

Dakota turned them into what little wind was left so Josh could take the sail down, and then they took an oar each and set to rowing the rest of the way. Side by side, they soon fell into an easy rhythm.

At the top end of the inlet, they headed toward

the old pilings left over from the days of the cement factory. Nesting boxes were attached to the tops of the pilings, and as they got closer they could hear the shrieking of dozens of baby birds hollering for food.

"They're purple martins," Dakota told Josh, ducking as one swooped especially low over her head. "In the winter, they migrate down to the Amazon. Can you imagine how far that is?"

Josh shook his head at the thought of such little birds flying so far. "They must have to eat a lot before they leave."

"Yes! I read that some birds have to double their body weight. But also, they have to time it just right with the weather and the winds. And they don't all make it."

Josh and Dakota sat for a few minutes more, watching the birds swooping and diving as they came and went from the nesting boxes, feeding their hungry babies.

"I can't wait to show all this to Matt," Josh said.

"It must be fun to have a brother." Dakota sounded wistful. "I don't have any siblings."

"Yeah, it's good. But he can be a pain sometimes too, like when his friends come over and he's trying to act all cool." And when Mom made him help Josh with his reading. "But mostly Matt's okay."

Thinking about reading, Josh fidgeted, toying with a loose thread on his life jacket. Later this afternoon he had his first reading lesson with Mrs. Gordon. Why had he agreed to it? Now he had to fit in lessons with two different tutors, on top of sailing practice! He wondered if there was any way he could get out of working with Mrs. Gordon. Maybe he could just get her talking about the Olympics and she would forget about the reading. Yeah, right. As if.

CHAPTER 16

Out of the Blue

With dread, Josh biked to Mrs. Gordon's for his first lesson. But this time, as he parked his bike in the backyard, he noticed a small brass cannon hidden between the big blue flower heads on the hydrangeas.

When Mrs. Gordon answered the door, Josh asked her about it.

"It was used for starting yacht races. When I saw it in an antique shop, it reminded me so much of sailing when I was a girl that I had to have it," Mrs. Gordon explained as she led him into the kitchen. "Shall we start with some iced tea?"

Josh nodded and took the glass she handed him. He wandered over to the birdcage, which was sitting under the window by the kitchen table. Charlie was hanging upside down from the top of the cage, flapping his wings for attention.

"Hello, Charlie," Josh said.

"Hello, hello, hello," Charlie parroted back.

"Do you remember Josh?" Mrs. Gordon asked the bird.

Josh laughed as Charlie nodded, ducking his head and looking at Josh from one eye.

Mrs. Gordon sat down at the kitchen table and absentmindedly scratched the bird's head through the bars before turning to Josh. "Tell me, how did you and Dakota meet?"

He explained how he'd planned to ask Matt to sail with him, but that Matt couldn't come.

"Oh, that's too bad," Mrs. Gordon said. "But I know Dakota is thrilled to have made a new friend." She smiled at Josh. "So tell me about Matt, does he like to read?"

Josh gulped at the change in topic, but he nodded. "He likes to read about computers and programming, and robotics."

"And what about your mom?"

"She reads lots of books for work."

"And your dad?"

"Mostly just boat-building and sailing magazines.

He says he wasn't that good at reading in school, either."

Mrs. Gordon sipped her iced tea and nodded, as though connecting the dots in a puzzle in her head.

"Sounds like your family doesn't read a lot of fiction?"

Josh shook his head and wiped at a dribble of condensation on the outside of his glass. "Mom says she doesn't have time for made-up stories, that the only way to advance at work is to stay current in her field and learn about the latest project-management techniques."

"She sounds like a very driven, capable sort of person," Mrs. Gordon said. "Not that there's anything wrong with that, but I think it's important to read for enjoyment too. Sometimes reading about characters in books can inspire us or help us see the world in a different way."

Josh hadn't thought of it that way, but then it was hard for him to imagine reading being anything except a struggle.

"Anyway, let's get started. Shall we sit on the couch?"

Feeling sick, Josh followed Mrs. Gordon to the living room.

"You're not going to tell Dakota, are you?" he asked.

"Of course not! It'll be our secret," she said. Then, producing a pile of slim books, she added, "I thought we'd start with graphic novels. Have you read these?"

Josh had heard of graphic novels, but they were still books, and he'd never been tempted to read one. Wondering what was special about them, he looked through the books Mrs. Gordon passed to him. Not surprisingly, none of them looked familiar. He shook his head.

"Well, choose one and we'll get started."

Josh's hand shook as he selected a book with a kid playing soccer on the cover.

"That's a good one," Mrs. Gordon said enthusiastically. She flipped it open and Josh was amazed to see that the pages were mostly pictures with just a few words, like comics but longer. "I'll read some to get us started. All right?"

Josh nodded, hands clenched in his lap.

Mrs. Gordon put on her glasses and began reading. She pointed at the pictures as she read and gave the characters different voices, so that soon Josh was caught up in the story, almost like a movie playing in his head.

But after a few pages, she stopped. "Your turn, young man. Just take your time. There's no hurry."

Josh froze. He tried to swallow the metallic taste in his mouth. He stammered his way through the first sentence with Mrs. Gordon helping him, and then the second sentence. But it was hard work. Even though there weren't many words on the page, the letters jiggled and some of the words just looked like blobs.

Josh felt the breath catch in his throat and the beginnings of a prickle behind his eyes. He was never going to be able to read. Why had he thought it would be any different with Mrs. Gordon?

For a while longer, they pressed on, with Mrs. Gordon gently helping him sound out the words and encouraging him to keep trying. But as time wore on, Josh sank lower and lower into the couch, wishing he could disappear.

Eventually, Mrs. Gordon put her hand on his shoulder. "Why don't you take a breather. I've got an idea." She went to the sideboard and slid open a drawer. When she came back to the couch, she had a collection of pieces of coloured plastic. "These are called overlays," she said. "Some people find that a particular colour helps them see words more clearly. Shall we try and see if they help?"

Josh nodded, but he was dubious. He didn't see how coloured plastic was going to magically make reading easier. One of his tutors in Ontario had tried to make him use an orange one once, but it hadn't helped at all.

Mrs. Gordon slid a purple overlay over the first line of words.

Josh squinted, but the words were still just a jumble of letters. "It doesn't look any different to me."

"Try this yellow one," Mrs. Gordon coaxed.

But if anything, the yellow made it worse. It was as if the words had turned into moths and flitted away altogether.

"How about this turquoise one?"

As she slid it across the page, Josh gaped.

"What?" Mrs. Gordon asked.

"The words... they're all lined up," Josh said. "Like they're in order." He slid his finger up to the first sentence and whispered the words to himself. There were still lots of words he didn't know, but... he stopped to think about it... if the words were in order and the blobs disappeared, maybe, just maybe, Mrs. Gordon really could help him.

For the first time, Josh felt the smallest flicker of hope.

CHAPTER 17

Look Out!

Over the next few weeks, Josh and Dakota spent most of their time together, either holed up in Dakota's turret, looking through the pictures in her books about racing tactics, or out on the water. Sometimes they each sailed their own boat, to practise race starts. On those days, Mrs. Gordon rowed out to meet them and pretended to be the committee boat, setting up the start line and sounding the starting horn, and then they would tack against each other up to Senanus Island. But mostly they both sailed in *Nomad* so that they could learn each other's strengths and weaknesses, as well as *Nomad's*.

One particularly fine day, when the sun was shining brightly and the wind was whipping up just a few whitecaps, they decided to sail the race course.

"Did you remember your hat?" Dakota asked Josh at the dinghy dock. She tugged her hat, a floppy one with a soft brim, onto her head. The previous day he'd forgotten his, and now his nose was a brilliant shade of red.

"Yeah." Josh pulled on his baseball cap. "Did you remember the chocolate?"

"What do you think?" Dakota plucked a bar from her bag and waved it teasingly in front of Josh.

Since the wind had swung around today, they sailed straight off the dock and headed toward Senanus Island. Whitecaps rolled away from them, and *Nomad* surged forward.

On the other side of the bay, a float plane turned into the inlet, dropping behind the trees and out of sight. Off to starboard, a pair of seagulls landed on a half-submerged log. One had its bill jammed open with two sea star legs sticking out.

Dakota grasped at her throat and made gagging noises, pretending to choke.

A gurgle escaped from Josh, and then another, until he was laughing so hard he doubled over, wheezing and gasping for breath.

Behind them the ferry sounded its horn as it left the pier, filled with cars headed for the bay on the other side of the inlet.

Josh made sure that they weren't in its path. Even though *Nomad* had the right of way because they were under sail, it wasn't smart to play chicken with the ferry.

As he turned back, a sail appeared at the entrance to the inlet. Josh cursed under his breath.

"What?" Dakota asked.

"It's Brittany!" Josh pointed at the sail heading in their direction. "Look how fast she's going."

"We can beat her," Dakota said. "Racing's about tactics, not just speed."

"Yeah, right." Josh knew that was true, in theory, but that didn't mean he really believed it in his gut.

"She's not even practising with her crew," Dakota said. "That's not smart."

"I guess not," said Josh, one eye still on the ferry.

As they got farther out in the bay and away from the shelter of the land, *Nomad* picked up speed. With the wind behind them, it didn't feel as if they were going fast. But by comparing their position against things on land, like the boat ramp and the clump of trees on the point, Josh could tell they were making headway.

Dakota sat by the daggerboard, hunched over the compass, peering at the dial.

Josh glanced back at Brittany. "Do you think she'll—"

"Oh, no!" Dakota yelled. "Look out!"

Josh spun around. "What?"

"There's a log! A deadhead!" Dakota pointed frantically at a half-submerged log floating in the water directly ahead of them. "Go to starboard!"

"Ready about!" Josh yelled. He pushed hard on the tiller to turn away from the log.

Dakota shoved the compass in her pocket and ducked as the boom swung across.

There was a loud thump, the crunch of splintering wood, and a groan. *Nomad* shuddered and stopped dead, jerking Josh off balance.

"Ow!" he howled as he landed in the bottom of the boat and banged his elbow.

Dakota scrambled forward. "There's water coming in!"

"Yikes!" Josh's heart hammered and his brain raced. "Quick, stuff something in the hole." But what? Josh thought about using his sweatshirt—too big. He looked under the seat, but the only thing there was his emergency bag, with nothing the right size in it.

In the meantime, water poured through the hole, filling the bottom of the boat. It seeped into Josh's shoes, chilling his toes, but he was too busy thinking to notice.

There had to be something they could use. And then he saw Dakota's hat, jammed over her curly hair. That was it! "Dakota, use your hat to plug the hole."

"Good idea!" Dakota whipped off her hat and wedged it in the hole, twisting the hat like a corkscrew until the water slowed to a trickle.

At that moment the ferry sounded its horn, a couple of short warning blasts.

Josh grabbed the plastic bottle, cut in the shape of a bailer, and thrust it at Dakota. "Here, you bail."

While Dakota scooped water out of *Nomad*, Josh untangled the lines. He turned the boat until a gust of wind filled the sail. They sped forward just in time.

"Hey, you kids, watch out!" The ferry captain shook his fist at them.

Once the ferry had passed, Josh swung *Nomad*

around into the wind, into irons, so that the sail flapped uselessly and brought them to a stop.

Dakota kept emptying the bailer over the side.

"Let me have a turn," Josh said, taking the bailer from her. He scooped and emptied, scooped and emptied, until the boat was mostly dry.

In the distance, Brittany's sail disappeared behind Senanus Island.

Josh turned *Nomad* back toward the marina. His arms ached. But worse than that, his stomach had twisted itself into a knot. Maybe Dad would be able to fix *Nomad*—but could he do it in time for the race?

CHAPTER 18

Patch Work

Back at the marina, Josh and Dakota dragged *Nomad* up the low concrete ramp beside the boatyard. Now that the boat was out of the water, the hole gaped at them, like the mouth of a sea monster, teeth made of splintered plywood.

When Dad joined them, he squatted down and studied the hole. "Mmm," he said, tapping his finger on his lip and tilting his head first one way, then the other. "Do you want the good news or the bad news first?" he asked.

Josh shrugged.

"Good news first," said Dakota, looking for the positive as always.

"Well, I can fix the hole," Dad said. "But I don't have time this week. We have to move that fishing boat off the ways on the next big tide, which is on Friday night. Sorry, kids."

Josh felt light-headed as Dad hurried back to his work. If Dad couldn't fix *Nomad*, he didn't know what he was going to do. It wasn't as if they could use Dakota's boat. It was just too small for the two of them to sail together.

He picked up a stone and pitched it into the water, and then another and another, watching them sink all the way to the bottom. "There must be something we can do...," he said. "Maybe we could fix *Nomad* ourselves?"

For once, Dakota looked dubious.

"Can you think of a better idea?" he demanded.

She shook her head. "We could try," she said, thinking it through. "I've helped Mom build model houses. It can't be much harder than that."

An hour later, after Dad had agreed to the plan and they'd got the supplies they needed from Dad's locker, Josh and Dakota staggered down the ramp, dragging a bucket of metal bar-clamps between them. When they reached *Nomad*, they dropped the bucket on the concrete and flopped down beside it. Zippy, who had followed them, stood watching with tongue hanging out and head tipped to one side.

Josh flexed his fingers. A dark purple line crossed the palm of his hand where the wire bucket handle had dug in. Even though the clamps were small, they were heavy. He rubbed at the line, but it didn't go away.

Glancing at his watch, Josh saw he had just two hours before he had to be at Mrs. Gordon's. So far he'd managed to keep his daily lessons with Dakota's nana a secret. Dad thought he was at Dakota's house, and Dakota thought he was doing his chores for Mike, and that was the way he intended to keep it. He jumped to his feet to get Dad.

Behind him, he heard the sound of flip-flops slapping across the concrete. He swung around in time to see Brittany examining *Nomad*. While he watched, she snapped a couple of pictures with her phone.

"What are you doing?" he growled, staring at her. "Spying on me?"

Brittany slid her sunglasses down over her eyes. "What happened?" she asked with fake concern.

Josh wanted to wipe that smug look off her face more than anything. He thrust his hands behind his back so she wouldn't see his fingers clenching.

"We hit a deadhead," Dakota said, standing beside Josh, hands on her hips. "But don't worry. We're going to fix the hole before the race."

"Oh, I wasn't worried," Brittany said airily. "Just keeping my eye on J-Josh here."

Just then, Dad arrived, a fresh streak of blue paint on his chin. He held a bundle of disposable brushes and sticks of varying lengths. He looked at Brittany. "Who's this?"

"Brittany," Josh muttered.

"Oh, from the Lodge?" Dad asked, recognition dawning.

Brittany nodded.

"Have you come to help?" Dad added the brushes and sticks to the bucket of clamps. He patted his pockets and pulled out a tape measure.

Josh snorted.

"I would love to help, but my father sent me over to get some papers from Mike," Brittany said, giving Dad the sugary smile she used on the teachers at school.

"You've got to be kidding," Josh snapped. "As if you'd help anyway."

Brittany's eyes widened. Seeming wounded, she glanced at Dad, waiting for him to defend her.

Dad looked from Josh to Brittany and back, his eyebrows raised.

Brittany sighed. Pursing her lips, she looked down at her phone and scrolled through the pictures. "Time for one more?" she asked. Without waiting for a reply, she snapped a photo of Josh and Dakota in front of *Nomad*. "See you later... Josh." She turned on her heel and stalked off.

Josh scowled. He watched her go right past Mike's office and up the stairs. Those pictures would be all over the Internet within minutes, and everyone was going to know he'd screwed up. What was wrong with him that he couldn't even sail his own boat without putting a hole in it? His fingernails dug into the palm of his hand as he tried to staunch the panic flooding through him. "I guess she didn't need those papers," he muttered.

Dad shot him an exasperated look but then got down to business, showing them how to clean the edges of the hole by scraping in the direction of the grain and how to round over the corners and edges of the patch with the sandpaper.

For the next hour, Josh and Dakota scraped and sanded while Zippy supervised. When their fingerprints had almost worn off, and the hole was free of splinters and the edges of the patch were smooth, it was time to mix the epoxy.

Josh pulled the page of instructions out from under the rubber band holding it against the side of the bottle. The words wriggled like a pile of mealworms. He put his finger on the page and waited. It didn't help that the letters were tiny. He stumbled through a few words but paused when he got to one he didn't recognize. He tried to sound it out without moving his lips, but it was no good.

He unclenched his teeth. "Here, read this and figure out how much resin and hardener we need," he said, passing the instructions to Dakota. "I'll get the mixing pots."

Dakota frowned and took the paper. "It says two pumps of resin and one pump of hardener."

"Yeah, that's what I thought," Josh said. He avoided Dakota's puzzled look and pulled one of the pots from the stack.

"Josh—"

"C'mon, let's mix the epoxy and stick the patch on." Josh twisted the pump on the resin until it unlocked. He did the same with the hardener.

Carefully, Dakota squirted the right amount of each into the pot.

Josh stirred it with a mixing stick until the coloured hardener disappeared into the clear resin. He set the pot down on the concrete and reached for the disposable brushes.

Zippy darted forward. Trembling with excitement, he nudged the pot with his nose. The pot jiggled and then flipped, spilling epoxy in a sticky stream down the concrete before rolling off the ramp into the water with a plop.

"Zippy!" Josh and Dakota yelled. But Zippy was gone, up the ramp and into Mike's office.

Dakota giggled.

Josh snickered, his bad mood dissipating. "That dog!" he said, reaching for another pot to mix a fresh batch.

When it was mixed, they brushed the epoxy along the edges of the hole and spread it all over the plywood patch. Then Dakota held the patch while Josh tightened the clamps along the edge, squeezing the patch tight against the side of the boat.

Josh sat back on his haunches and heaved a sigh of relief. "We did it!"

Dakota cheered. "High five!"

CHAPTER 19

Chocolate Chip Cookies

After Josh said goodbye to Dakota, he gave her a long head start, then jumped onto his bike and pedalled to Mrs. Gordon's. When he knocked on Mrs. Gordon's door, she shouted for him to come in.

"Thank goodness you're here."

Josh stepped into the kitchen. It looked like *Jeanette*'s galley the time he and Dad had been caught in a storm in the strait. Bowls, spoons, and plastic containers sat higgledy-piggledy on the counter, and a fine layer of flour covered everything, including Mrs. Gordon's hair.

"Hello, hello, hello," the parrot chirped from his cage in the corner.

"Charlie, be a good bird. Be quiet," Mrs. Gordon said.

"Good bird, good bird, good bird," Charlie cackled.

"I'm in the middle of baking some cookies," she said to Josh. "Can you help me? The recipe's on the table. How much butter do we need?"

Josh slouched over to the table and sat on the edge of a chair. A huge red and white cookbook lay open on the table, the paper dotted with oily spots.

He was worn out from all the scraping and sanding, but he dutifully slipped the turquoise overlay out of his bag and slid it over the words on the page. With the overlay in place he could read the large words at the top of the page. "Chocolate Chip Cookies." Yum! He slid his finger and the overlay down the page, muttering the words to himself. "Butter... here it is," he said. "It says *100*."

"*100*?" Mrs. Gordon looked over her shoulder. "What does it say after *100*?"

Josh squinted at the page. "Baking powder?" he asked.

"No, no," Mrs. Gordon laughed. "The measurement. Is it grams or millilitres or..."

Josh stared at the page, his ears burning.

"Take it slowly, Josh. You're doing fine. Is there

a letter after the *100*? Sometimes cookbooks use abbreviations."

He looked again, and sure enough, there was a letter. But which letter was it? "A *g*?" he asked.

"That must be it. It's a *g*, for grams. So we need one hundred grams of butter. Let's cut some off the block. You can wash your hands at the kitchen sink."

Josh did as he was told.

"Grab that knife and cut off a slice, will you? And put it on the scales here." She indicated a flat plastic scale with a digital panel on the front.

Josh used the knife to carry the slice of butter from the chopping board to the scale.

"Tell me what the scale says," Mrs. Gordon said. "Then can you pull up my sleeves? I seem to have got myself in a terrible mess here."

Josh read the numbers on the panel. "65?" he asked. He tugged at the sleeves on her cardigan until they were above her elbows.

Mrs. Gordon lifted her arm up and brushed her hair back from her face. "We'll need more than that," she said. "Cut off another bit."

Once again, Josh sliced off some butter and added it to the scale. This time the scale read *102*.

"Near enough. It's art, not science." Mrs. Gordon

picked up the butter with her fingers and added it to the sugar in the bowl.

Josh stood on his toes and peered into the bowl. "What are you doing?"

"Creaming the butter and sugar." She kept stirring and pressing with a wooden spoon until the butter and sugar mixture was pale and creamy. "Right, what's next?"

Josh scooted back to the cookbook and ran his finger down the list. "Cream the butter..." When he came to the next word, he looked up at the windowsill where clay shapes he and Mrs. Gordon had made of all the letters of the alphabet sat in a row. He found the letters for this word and sounded it out. "And...," he said. Mrs. Gordon was right. The clay shapes really did help him remember the letters. "...sugar."

"Very good, Josh. Yes, that's what we've just done. What's next?"

Josh looked at the next step. "Mix the re... remaining in... gre... dients."

"Well done! Will you read out the other things in the list?"

As he read them out, he watched Mrs. Gordon tip them into the bowl one by one.

"I think we have everything. Can you help me stir?" She brought the bowl over to the table, and Josh stirred and stirred until everything was mixed. It looked much tastier than the cookie dough Mom used to squeeze out of the tube at home.

Next, they spooned the mixture onto baking sheets, and Josh squished the blobs flat with a fork.

"They need about twenty-five minutes to bake," Mrs. Gordon said as she set the timer. "So that gives us just enough time to read some more of *Swallows and Amazons.*"

Josh nodded.

Mrs. Gordon carried in the clay shapes and set them on the table in the living room. Then she and Josh settled on the sofa together, with the book resting on Josh's knee and the overlay at the ready.

Charlie sat on his perch, preening quietly.

For a moment, the familiar panic made Josh's heart race. But soon the beating slowed down. Sitting beside Mrs. Gordon was like being out on the water in *Nomad.* It was nothing like reading with the tutor at the library, with the kids from school walking past the window and staring at him.

For the next twenty minutes, they read a few pages of *Swallows and Amazons.* Whenever Josh

119

struggled, Mrs. Gordon placed her hand on his arm and talked about what was happening in the story until his breathing slowed and he could read the words.

When the timer rang, Mrs. Gordon closed the book. "That's enough for today," she said. "Let's take the cookies out before they burn."

In the kitchen, she slid the hot baking sheet out of the oven and onto the counter.

Josh helped move the cookies to the cooling rack.

Then they sat at the table, nibbling hot cookies and talking about the book and what John's dad had meant about duffers and drowning.

"Basically, what he means is that he trusts them to be careful," Mrs. Gordon said.

"And to not drown themselves," Josh added.

Mrs. Gordon nodded, wiping her fingers on her apron. "Well, I have to say, you did a great job today," she said. "And I really appreciated your help with the cookies."

Josh shrugged, trying to act cool, but he couldn't help smiling back at her.

CHAPTER 20

Confession

A few mornings later, Josh woke up with the sheets tangled around his legs. All night he'd had nightmares about Brittany imitating him, jabbing her finger at a page, mockingly sounding the words out. Even though he was getting better at reading, he still couldn't imagine standing up in front of a group and reading out loud. Especially if the group included Brittany.

He kicked the sheets aside.

Dad had left for work already, so Josh grabbed an apple and a couple of cheese slices from the fridge. He stuffed his feet into his sneakers, threw his backpack on, and slipped outside. The air was crisp and fresh and made him want to shake himself all over like Zippy.

He rolled the cheese slices into a tube and chewed on them as he walked through the marina, up to the boatyard.

At the picnic table, Dakota was writing in an exercise book.

"What are you writing?" Josh asked as he swung a leg over the bench and sat down next to her.

"A story about a dog called Zippy." Dakota angled the paper so he could see. At the top of the page, she'd doodled a picture of Zippy with the mixing pot balanced on his nose.

Josh grinned. She'd got Zippy's expression just right.

"So, what do we do next?" Dakota asked.

"We need to see if the epoxy has set." From his perch at the table, Josh eyed *Nomad*.

The boat was sitting at the bottom of the ramp where they'd left her, with the patch clamped to the inside. But something was different.

Josh leapt off the bench and dashed down to *Nomad* for a closer look. Two days earlier there had been a ragged crater on the outside of the hull, but now there was a gleaming blob of thickened epoxy. He poked his finger at the epoxy. It was hard. "Dad must have filled this in yesterday," he said.

Next to *Nomad*, a can of paint, a paintbrush, and some fresh sandpaper sat on the concrete. A note was wedged under the paint.

Josh tugged it out and smoothed it against his leg. He tried to pretend that Dakota wasn't there. But it was no use. The words wriggled and jumped on the page, like salmon trying to swim upstream. The good feelings from earlier in the week dissolved in a flash.

"What does it say?" Dakota asked, leaving her paper and pencils on the table and coming down the ramp to stand beside him.

"I don't know," he growled. "I can never read Dad's writing." If he'd had the turquoise overlay in his pocket he might have tried it, but it was in his bag up at the picnic table, and anyway, it was one thing to use it when he was reading with Mrs. Gordon, but something entirely different to use it in front of Dakota. Instead, he thrust the page at her.

Dakota took a step back, looking concerned. "Josh... is everything all right?"

"What do you think?" Concern was the one thing he couldn't handle right now, with the pressure of making sure *Nomad* was fixed and keeping the lessons with Mrs. Gordon a secret. Everything he'd kept

123

hidden for so long suddenly boiled to the surface. "If we don't win the race, I have to read at the library on Literacy Day in front of everyone," he said. "I *suck* at reading. Like, basically, I *can't* read. Okay? Now you know." He hung his head and squeezed his eyes shut, not wanting to see the look on her face.

He could imagine it anyway. He'd seen the same look hundreds of times before. The smirks, the whispers and nudges, the giggling behind hands, and, worst of all, the sniggering out loud in front of him. As if he couldn't see and hear them laughing at him. Seeing the little kids look at him like that, kids who were half his age and already reading better than he was—that would be more than he could take.

"But you read the newspaper articles," Dakota said, sounding confused.

"Yeah, but…"

"And you read the poster about the race."

"Well…"

"And you read the instructions for mixing the epoxy. Didn't you?"

"It's not easy for me. You don't get it." Josh knew he was sulking, but he couldn't help it. Why was it that no one understood? Not Mom, not Dad. Not even Dakota. "When I try to read, the words jump around on the page, and some of the letters look backwards. Sometimes even if I concentrate, the letters won't sit still."

"Oh. You've got dyslexia? Why didn't you say so? My dad's dyslexic."

Josh kept staring at the ground, going over it in his head. She wasn't laughing at him. He glanced up, still half expecting to see a smirk on her face.

Instead, she looked straight at him with a determined expression. "Don't worry about it. We're going to win."

Josh wanted to believe her. "We are?"

"Of course! We're a team." Dakota chewed on her fingernail for a moment. "Maybe Nan could help you with reading. She taught me."

Josh coughed. "She is," he muttered.

"Did she make cookies?"

Josh caught the gleam in her eyes. He remembered the bag of cookies Mrs. Gordon had slid into his pack after his last lesson.

"Chocolate chip?" Dakota continued.

Josh glanced at his bag. How did she know? Could she smell them? "You can't have any until we're finished!" He snatched Dad's note back and dared the words to jump around. This time they all sat side by side, and Josh was able to read the directions, one at a time. "Dad says to sand the epoxy on the outside of the hull until it's smooth and then give it two coats of paint, one this morning and one tomorrow."

Dakota bent down to pick up the wooden block and piece of sandpaper. She set to work sanding the lump of epoxy that filled the hole. A fine layer of dust floated down the ramp.

While she did that, Josh took the clamps off the patch on the inside of the boat and made sure it was glued firmly in place. It was.

When they were finished with the sanding, Josh pried open the can of paint with a screwdriver.

"Is that deck paint?" Dakota asked, pointing at the deck chair on the label.

Josh nodded. "Dad says it's just as good as marine enamel, but much cheaper." The paint was a dark blue, the same colour as *Nomad*'s hull. It looked well mixed, but Josh stirred it, just to be sure. When he was done, he dipped the brush in and swiped paint across the epoxy, covering the bare patch until he couldn't see where the hole had been.

When he'd finished, he put the brush aside and sat back to admire the job they'd done.

Dakota cheered. "Looks good. Can we have the cookies now?"

"Yeah. But don't tell anyone about the reading," Josh said gravely. "Okay? Swear!"

"I swear," Dakota said solemnly. Then, breaking into laughter, she yelled, "Race you to the cookies!"

CHAPTER 21

Wind Warning

The day of the race finally arrived. Early that morning, Josh sat on the deck of the *Jeanette*, his feet wedged against the rail. A strip of sunlight angled across the bow, but the wind had come up and the boat shifted uncomfortably in the swells. Josh's guts churned, but not because of the weather.

He munched his toast and watched the seagulls squabbling over a paper bag that had fallen from the garbage bin. One grabbed a hamburger wrapper out of the bag and flew away with it, squawking with triumph. Another followed, screaming, "Mine, mine, mine!"

Josh kept them in sight until he saw Dakota striding along the dock toward him.

She clambered aboard, brandishing a newspaper. "Did you read the forecast?"

"Why?"

"There's a small-craft warning."

"No way!" Heart pounding, he leapt to his feet.

"They'll have to cancel the race," Dakota said. She helped herself to Josh's other piece of toast. "Ewww! Is this lemon marmalade? You can have it back."

"Let's listen to the marine forecast," he said. With the *Jeanette* swaying against the dock, he held on to the handrail as he scrambled down into the cabin.

Dakota followed and sat on the bottom step.

"Hi, kids," Dad said. He poured himself a cup of coffee and put the coffee pot back on the stove.

Josh perched on the edge of the chair at the chart table. "Dad, if there's a small-craft warning, do you think they'll cancel the race?"

"I guess they might postpone it until tomorrow or next weekend." Dad sipped his coffee.

Like the two-stroke engine on *Jeanette*'s tender, Josh's brain ticked over. If they postponed the race long enough, he wouldn't have to read on Literacy Day, next Saturday. He turned the radio on and flipped to the station with the weather updates.

129

"...winds gusting up to gale force later this morning...," the announcer was saying.

Josh hugged his knees to his chest, trying to squash the hope that had bubbled to the surface.

Just then there were footsteps outside on the dock.

"Knock, knock," a voice called.

Dakota jumped to her feet. "Nan? Is that you?" She stood on the top step and poked her head out.

Josh climbed up beside her. Sure enough, it was Mrs. Gordon, with a tin of cookies and a large white parcel under her arm.

"Permission to come aboard?" Mrs. Gordon asked.

"Of course! Welcome aboard, Mrs. Gordon," Josh said, waving her toward the carpeted steps they used to climb onto the boat.

When Mrs. Gordon stepped into the cabin, her eyes lit up. "What a beautiful home you've created!"

"Mrs. Gordon," Dad said, offering her his hand. "It's a pleasure to see you again. Josh says you've been helping them get ready for the race?"

Mrs. Gordon looked at Josh, but he shook his head slightly so she'd know to keep quiet about the reading lessons. She smiled back at him, a secret twinkle in her eye just for him. "Yes, I've been helping them, but they've done all the hard work themselves. I've never seen a more dedicated pair."

Then she turned to include Dakota. "I've got a surprise for you two," she said, holding out the white parcel. "A friend of mine had this old sail lying around, and I thought you could use it. I've seen how hard you've worked to get ready for the race, so I asked my friend to cut it down to the right size for *Nomad.*"

Josh gasped. A real sail to replace the blue tarp! "Thanks, Mrs. Gordon." He stroked the cloth and beamed.

"You're the best!" Dakota flung her arms around her nana.

Mrs. Gordon kissed her lightly on the head.

"Let's try it out," Josh said, heading for the deck. And then he stopped. Outside, the wind howled and shrieked. He threw his hands up, cursing.

"Josh," Dad said reprovingly.

Josh dipped his head. "Sorry."

"Actually," Mrs. Gordon said, patting him on the shoulder, "today's the perfect day to try out this sail. It's got three sets of reef points, so when the wind's really blowing, you can make the sail smaller.

Nomad will go a little slower, but you'll have more control. Come with me. I'll show you." She picked up the sail and led them outside.

At *Nomad*, Josh unthreaded the blue tarp and laced the new sail along the yard and the boom, struggling as the wind tried to jerk the sail out of his hands. He and Dakota pulled the sail partway up the mast, and then Mrs. Gordon showed them how to tie reef knots along the foot of the sail.

"See how it reduces the sail area?" she said as they finished hoisting the sail.

Josh nodded.

By now, other people had begun arriving for the race. Kids shouted at each other as they got their boats ready while their parents stood in huddles, shaking hands and catching up with friends. Sails and halyards clanked and creaked in the wind.

There were lots of kids Josh didn't recognize, but Daniel was there with his little brother Alex, and a couple of girls from school. He saw them looking at him and pointing, but he pretended not to notice.

At the end of the dock, Mike stood beside a woman in a red suit. He called for attention and gestured with both hands for everyone to be quiet.

Josh squinted at the woman. She looked familiar,

but he couldn't remember where he'd seen her before.

"Hello, everyone!" Mike's voice boomed across the crowd. "Welcome to the first annual Senanus Island Small Boat Race. Our sponsor, Mrs. Johanna Lambert from the Arbutus Bay Lodge and Spa, is here to show her support."

Brittany's mother! Josh groaned. She couldn't rig the race, could she?

"Welcome!" Brittany's mother spoke into a megaphone. "I know you're all wondering if we'll be racing today since there was a small-craft warning this morning. I'm happy to announce that the wind has dropped enough for the race to go ahead as planned." She paused while everyone cheered. "But it's still very windy, so be careful. Have fun and be safe!"

Josh let out the breath he'd been holding. There was no turning back now. They'd just have to do their best. He turned to Dakota. "Are you ready?"

"Aye aye, Captain!"

CHAPTER 22

A Risky Decision

Josh and Dakota hurried back to *Nomad* to finish getting ready.

All along the dock, kids pulled on their windbreakers and life jackets and made their final preparations.

Josh went through his checklist. Flashlight, whistle, knife, first aid kit, emergency rations, drinking water, dry clothing, bailer—check, check, check. Then he looked over his shoulder to make sure Dad and Mrs. Gordon weren't looking. When he saw that they weren't, he quickly started undoing the reef knots.

"What are you doing?" Dakota asked.

"I'm taking out the reef knots. With more sail area we might have a chance of winning."

"Do you think that's a good idea? It's really windy." Dakota sounded uncertain.

Normally Josh would have agreed, but for once he was sick of playing it safe. If there was a chance they could win, it was worth the risk, wasn't it? He chewed on his lip and kept attacking the knots. "I want to win, don't you?"

"Of course!" Dakota shot back as another gust of wind rattled the sail, and water sprayed across the dock. "But we're not going to win if we capsize!"

She had a point, Josh thought, but then he remembered Brittany's smug looks and nasty comments. "We won't capsize," he said crossly. "I know what I'm doing."

"Yes, I know," Dakota said. "But Nan said we'd have more control if we reef the sail. Maybe we should use the first set of reef points?" She pulled a floating cord out of her pocket and attached the ends to her glasses before putting them back on. "We'll still go faster than we would have with the old sail," she reasoned.

Josh scowled. Now was not the time for compromise. He'd made up his mind... hadn't he? Images swirled through his head as he tried to picture all the different scenarios. Speed or control—which would give them the edge?

As the wind howled and the choppy water pummelled *Nomad*, Josh had to agree that Dakota was right, as usual. More control might give them a better chance against Brittany.

Chewing his lip, he retied the reef knots using the first set of points, hoping he was making the best decision.

Just as he was finishing, Dad and Mrs. Gordon arrived at the dinghy.

"You kids all set?" Dad asked.

Josh and Dakota looked at each other.

"I guess so," Dakota said, quirking her eyebrow at Josh in a silent question—*are we?*

He nodded. "We're ready."

"Good luck," Mrs. Gordon said. "And have fun! That's what's important."

After quick hugs all round, Josh and Dakota scrambled aboard *Nomad* and Dad pushed them off.

Josh sailed out to the start line, where a dozen boats milled around. It was nothing like the club races in Toronto, where everyone sailed in the same type of boat. Here, the boats were all different shapes and sizes—some wooden, some plastic, and some fibreglass. In the chop, *Nomad* felt like a ride at the fair. One minute they were cresting the top of a wave, and the next they'd dropped into a trough. Josh's stomach lurched with every descent. Nervously, he grimaced at Dakota, whose face matched the green of the water.

The most important thing now was not to cross the start line before the horn. So Josh circled around, making sure to stay out of the way of the other boats.

Just as he was looking over his shoulder to see if he could spot Brittany, Dakota yelled, "Watch out!"

Brittany sliced across their bow, so close that she could have reached out and touched them. She cast a superior look in their direction as Josh nudged the tiller aside just in time to avoid a collision.

Josh hunched his shoulders until he remembered Mrs. Gordon's instructions to relax. He rolled his shoulders, releasing some of the tension, and decided Mrs. Gordon was right. He had to forget about Brittany and concentrate fully on what he was doing.

Dakota gave him the thumbs-up. The air horn sounded. Then they were off, racing toward Senanus Island.

CHAPTER 23

Winners and Losers

Josh and Dakota tacked back and forth toward the first buoy, Josh at the tiller and Dakota perched up front. Choppy waves slapped the side of the boat, and every so often a tall one sprayed over *Nomad*'s bow. They'd got a good start, but Brittany and her crewmate, Amber, had pushed to the front, with Daniel and Alex close behind.

On every tack, Brittany and Amber edged ahead, their bigger sail catching more wind and their fibreglass hull slicing through the water like a shark's fin.

Josh leaned forward in his seat, willing *Nomad* to go faster. "C'mon, c'mon," he murmured.

Brittany and Amber led them round the first buoy, two boat lengths ahead of Daniel and Alex, three

ahead of Josh and Dakota. With the wind beh
them now, they had a straight run toward Senar
Island, which gave Josh an idea.

"Let's pull up the daggerboard," he said.

"Aye aye, Captain." Dakota tugged on the boar
until it slid out of the water. Without the extra drag
Nomad instantly picked up speed.

Josh brightened. "That's more like it."

Up ahead, Brittany and Amber switched places,
and Brittany pulled out another sail.

"She's crazy," Dakota said. "A spinnaker in this
wind?"

Josh agreed. But he wondered if he'd made a mis-
take using the reef points and making *Nomad*'s sail
smaller.

As they neared Senanus Island, Brittany surged
farther ahead. The spinnaker was definitely giving
her extra speed.

There had to be a way to outsmart her. Josh thought
about it. On the last leg, they'd be tacking into the
wind again, and she wouldn't be able to use the
spinnaker. If he sailed close to the island, he might
be able to cut in front of her while she was pulling
it in. "Get ready to release the daggerboard," he told
Dakota and explained his plan.

Ahead of them, it looked as if Daniel had the same idea. He was angling in close to the island too.

Josh waited until the right moment. "Now."

Dakota dropped the daggerboard and *Nomad* slowed.

"Ready to jibe?"

"Ready."

Josh pushed the tiller, the boom swung over, Dakota ducked, and they passed Brittany.

"It worked!" Dakota shouted with glee.

Josh smirked as Brittany fished her spinnaker out of the water.

On this leg, the blustery wind made it harder to stay on course. Josh held the tiller as steady as he could while *Nomad* swooped and wheeled like a gull.

Dakota clung to the side with both hands.

Just ahead, Daniel and Alex tacked across *Nomad*'s bow, so close that Josh almost rammed them.

"Hey, watch out!" Daniel yelled.

Josh growled but held his line. If he could keep on this heading for another minute, they might have the advantage next time they crossed paths with Daniel.

Or not.

As a squall whipped across the bay, *Nomad* leaned into the wind, seawater streaming over the side. Josh eased the mainsheet and Dakota bailed while *Nomad* trembled, fighting to come upright.

Brittany's boat swerved as another gust buffeted them, but together she and Amber wrangled the boat under control.

Daniel wasn't so lucky. His boat keeled over, pitching Alex overboard, headfirst into the icy swells.

Josh shot Dakota a look of triumph. The finish line was just a dozen boat lengths away. They were going to make it. They were going to win! He would not have to read at the library. Relief flooded through him.

As they sailed on, Daniel's boat turned turtle, until it was completely upside down. Only the white hull was visible. Josh felt a pang of sympathy for Daniel and Alex. Being in the water in this weather would not be much fun. For a split second he considered helping them. But the buzz of the rescue Zodiac meant help was coming, and he could see Daniel swimming toward Alex.

Josh turned away only to find Brittany's eyes locked on him like a pair of tractor beams, preventing him from escaping. He tore his eyes from hers and concentrated on *Nomad* as they raced for the finish line.

"Help!" Daniel's voice was barely audible behind them over the shriek of the wind. "Somebody, help!"

Josh glanced over his shoulder. Daniel had reached Alex and was trying to keep his head above the waves. Alex flailed his arms and legs, dragging Daniel under the water with him.

"Josh," Dakota yelled. "Brittany's catching us."

Josh looked longingly at the finish line. All his instincts told him to go for it. He was so close. And Daniel was such a jerk.

"Help!" Daniel wailed, sounding frantic. Waves were rolling over them, one after another, and the brothers were clinging to each other.

Josh's mind whirled. If he went back to help them, he'd lose the race. He'd have to face the kids at the library, the giggles and smirks. And Brittany. Sneering.

Alex and Daniel disappeared under the waves again and came up spluttering and gasping. There wasn't time to wait for the Zodiac, and the other racers were far behind and struggling themselves. He and Dakota exchanged a look and she sent him a brief nod.

"Ready about," he yelled.

"Ready."

Swiftly, he pushed the tiller and turned *Nomad* around.

Dakota groaned. "We were this close to winning." She held up her fingers to show just how close.

Josh nodded glumly. "I know."

As they sailed back toward Daniel's overturned boat, Brittany flew by. "Loser!" she yelled, while beside her, Amber wore a guilty look.

Josh ignored the lurch in his gut. "Dakota, can you steer?"

"Sure." She scooted into Josh's place and grabbed hold of the tiller.

Josh yanked his shoes off and dived into the water. The cold took his breath away, but he ignored it and took a couple of strong strokes over to Daniel, whose teeth were chattering.

"Help!" Alex cried, grabbing hold of Josh's arm as water splashed in his face. "My foot's caught." Coughing and spluttering, he swallowed more water.

Daniel tried to keep him calm.

Josh tore his life jacket off. "Hold this," he ordered Alex. Then he dived under the water.

When his eyes adjusted, he could see a rope tangled around Alex's ankle. He tugged at it, but it refused to come loose. He kicked his way back to the surface and sucked in some air.

Alex choked as another wave swept over him. The buoyancy of the extra life jacket was barely keeping his head above the water.

Think, think, think, Josh told himself. As another wave rolled over them, the knife banged against his leg. The knife! He dragged it from the sheath and opened the biggest blade.

Alex's eyes grew as big as clamshells. Daniel looked relieved.

"It'll be okay," Josh yelled, his legs pedalling madly, treading water. He took a deep breath and dived under again, this time with the knife in his hand. He yanked at the rope and sawed frantically. Finally, one thread broke, and another, until he'd sliced all the way through.

Lungs bursting, Josh shot to the surface where Alex and Daniel were waiting.

"Thanks, dude," Daniel said, grabbing him by the shoulder. "You saved our butts."

Josh shrugged. His heart was pounding and his ears were ringing from holding his breath for so long.

"Let's get out of the water. It's freezing." He tugged them toward *Nomad*. With Dakota's help, he hoisted them into the boat, then scrambled aboard himself.

The rescue boat buzzed alongside *Nomad*. "You kids all right?" Mike asked. "Can you make it back to the dock?"

Josh nodded.

"Good lad. Here, wrap yourselves in this," Mike said, throwing over a silver space blanket. With a nod at Josh, he turned the Zodiac and sped off to help another capsized boat.

Alex and Daniel sat hunched in the bottom of *Nomad*, shivering.

Dakota wrapped the two of them in the space blanket and rubbed Alex's hands to warm them. Meanwhile, Josh hoisted the sail with freezing, shaking hands and got them underway.

When they crossed the finish line, a loud cheer erupted from the crowd watching the race. Wearing windbreakers and jackets in a rainbow of colours, they waved and called out to Josh and Dakota, Daniel and Alex.

At the dock, Brittany stood with her arms crossed and a smug look on her face. "Told you I'd win," she said.

Brittany's mom elbowed her aside and helped them climb out of *Nomad*. "Nice work," she said gruffly to Josh. She wrapped Alex in a wool blanket and steered him and Daniel away to find their parents.

The crowd pressed in closer around Josh and Dakota.

"Congratulations!"

"Well done!"

"Good job!"

Josh's cheeks burned. Eyes darting toward Dakota, he took a step backwards, wanting to get away from all the fuss.

Dad draped his jacket over Josh's shoulders and pulled him into a hug. "I'm so proud of you," he said. "You too, Dakota. I could see it from here. You didn't even hesitate."

Josh felt a stab of guilt at that. He *had* hesitated.

"Yes, well done, you two," Mrs. Gordon said.

Mike pushed his way through the crowd and shook Josh's hand. "Bravo, old chap. Great job out there."

Josh ducked his head and glanced away. He saw Brittany standing apart from everyone else, scowling at him.

"See you at the library," she mouthed.

CHAPTER 24

Facing Dad

Back at the *Jeanette*, Dad put a pot of coffee on the stove while Josh, still shivering, changed out of his wet clothes. With his back to Josh, Dad asked quietly, "What was that with Brittany back there? I saw her say something to you."

Josh shrugged. "Oh, that? Nothing." He avoided looking at Dad because he really didn't want to have this conversation.

"It didn't look like nothing."

Sighing, Josh perched at the table and helped himself to a cookie out of Mrs. Gordon's tin.

"Josh?"

"I made a bet with Brittany about the race," he mumbled. "Since I didn't win, I have to read out loud at the library on Literacy Day."

Dad sat down next to him. "A bet? You'd better tell me the whole story."

So Josh explained what had happened, how the book had fallen out of his bag at the library, and how Brittany had called *Nomad* a homemade bathtub and said that his blue tarp sail was lame. "I just wanted to prove that she was wrong, Dad."

"I see," Dad said quietly. "I wish you'd told me."

Josh shrugged again. "I can handle it," he said. "Anyway, I'm reading much better now. I've been having lessons with Mrs. Gordon as well as the tutor at the library. Mrs. Gordon gave me this coloured overlay, and when I put it over the words they all sit in a line in order." Josh pulled out the overlay and Dakota's now very battered copy of *Swallows and Amazons* and showed Dad how he laid the coloured plastic over the words. "Mrs. Gordon says that there's no scientific evidence that the overlays work, but if it helps me, I should use it."

"It sounds like Mrs. Gordon is pretty smart." Dad rested his hand on Josh's shoulder. "Kiddo, I'm really proud of you, and I know your mom will be too."

At the mention of Mom, Josh spluttered and grabbed another cookie. "You're not going to make me go back to Toronto, are you?" He was surprised to realize how much he'd grown to like it here with Dad and Dakota and Mrs. Gordon.

"Of course not. I was hoping you'd think of this as your home now. I know it's a little unconventional, but I think we make a great team."

Josh grinned. "I think so too!"

Dad was quiet for a moment, and then he said, "But you know your mom misses you, right?"

"I doubt it," Josh muttered under his breath. "She couldn't wait to get rid of me." He pulled one of his sketchbooks off the shelf and started doodling.

"Oh, Josh, that's not true. I know I've said some things about your mom that maybe I shouldn't have, but she really does want the best for you, just like I do. We both thought a different environment would be good for you, fewer distractions and a smaller class at school, but it was my idea that you come out here. She wasn't trying to get rid of you."

Josh bit his lip. "Really?" he asked in a small voice. "I thought she was mad at me."

"She wasn't mad. She was frustrated because she wanted to help you, but she didn't know how."

Josh leaned his head against Dad's shoulder. "So I can stay here with you?"

"Of course you can!" And Josh found himself being pulled into a big Dad bear hug.

CHAPTER 25

The Finish Line

The following Saturday, Josh slid his bike into the rack outside the library. He chewed the inside of his cheek as he did up the lock. Even though he'd practised his reading with Mrs. Gordon every day since the race, and he'd even started writing and drawing a graphic novel version of *Swallows and Amazons,* right now he felt as though he'd swallowed a wriggly bait worm.

When he pushed the library door open, the first thing he heard was Brittany's voice.

"I told you I'd win," she was saying.

A group of kids stood near the librarian's desk. Daniel and Alex were there, and Amber, as well as some other kids from their class.

Josh sidled up to the pillar, staying out of sight.

Now that he was here, he wished he hadn't come. Yeah, he'd lost the bet, but who cared about a stupid bet anyway? He could have just gone out sailing in *Nomad*.

"Well, look who's here!" Brittany said snidely.

Josh stepped out from behind the pillar and faced the group. Squaring his shoulders, he pretended he was John, captain of the *Swallow*, with his crew right behind him. John would know how to deal with Brittany.

"What are you going to read, J-Josh? Let me guess... a picture book?"

Josh cringed, but he stood his ground, looking each of the kids in the eye, daring them to laugh at him, just as he imagined John would do.

Daniel studied his shoes, refusing to make eye contact.

"I'm going to read a few pages of *Swallows and Amazons*," Josh said. His voice shook a little as he said the words.

Brittany snorted. "Really?"

"Really," he said firmly, trying to ignore the squirming bait worm.

For a moment there was silence. And then Daniel stepped forward, his eyes darting from Brittany to

Josh. "That's a good book," he said. He tugged Alex to stand with him next to Josh.

Brittany shot Daniel an incredulous look.

Daniel gave a half-shrug and pulled a copy of *Swallows and Amazons* from his bag.

Josh couldn't believe it.

Just then Dakota bounded up, hair bouncing and a smile spreading from ear to ear. "Have you signed in, Josh?"

"Not yet."

"Well, let's go." She seemed oblivious to Brittany, who was standing with her arms folded and lips pursed, tapping her foot.

Josh shrugged and started to walk away with Dakota, but Brittany stalked over to him and dragged him aside until it was just the two of them.

She put her face into his until all he could see were the spiky metal braces on her teeth. "You know I would have won anyway, even if you hadn't stopped to help Daniel and Alex." She seemed determined that he admit it.

"Who cares?" Josh said. "It's just a race." And he realized, with surprise, he meant it. Who'd have thought? Just eight weeks ago, winning the race was the only thing on his mind. Now he knew there were many more important things to focus on, like his friendship with Dakota and not giving up on reading, even when it seemed he'd never get any better at it. "Not everything is about winning."

Brittany's mouth hung open in a giant O. "Of course it is. Winning is everything."

"Is that what your parents say?" Josh threw back at her.

Brittany scowled at him. "Yes," she said sharply. "Dad says there are winners and losers in life. And that's what you are, Josh, a loser."

Josh flinched, but he stood firm. "And what if Alex had died? Would winning still be everything?"

Brittany paled and took a step backward. "Well—"

"Get a clue, Brittany." He shook his head. "For someone so smart, you just don't get it, do you?" He turned his back on her and walked toward Dakota, Daniel, and Alex. He almost expected her to follow, but when he glanced back, she was standing in the same spot, sniffling and texting on her phone.

At the desk in the children's section, the librarian was taking names. Josh and Dakota stood in line with the other kids who were volunteering to read. When Josh got to the desk, the librarian leaned forward and smiled warmly at him.

"Which time slot would you like?" she asked.

"Josh wants to go first," Dakota said, elbowing him.

"I do?"

"You do."

He gulped. "Josh Parker," he told the librarian.

She wrote his name in purple marker on her sheet. "Perfect! See you back here at eleven."

Dakota gave her name to the librarian as well, and then they went to find Mrs. Gordon, who had been waylaid when she ran into friends she played Scrabble with on Thursday nights.

When she'd finished chatting with her friends, the three of them headed for the comfortable chairs by the windows. There, Mrs. Gordon kept them entertained and distracted with stories of sailing adventures she'd had when she was a child.

Just before eleven o'clock they trooped back to the children's area.

The librarian had placed a small chair in front of a pile of brightly coloured cushions, and she was calling everyone over.

Josh shuffled his feet. It was time. His heart was hammering so loudly, he barely noticed that Dad had arrived.

Mrs. Gordon spoke his name. "Josh?"

He couldn't catch his breath and his lungs felt as if they might burst, but as soon as Mrs. Gordon put her hand on his shoulder, his chest stopped heaving.

"Remember, there's no need to hurry," she said.

Josh nodded and swigged some water from his drink bottle. "I'm fine," he said, pretending to himself that he was.

Clapping her hands, the librarian waited until everyone was quiet. "Let's get started. First, we have Josh reading from his favourite book."

Dad squeezed his shoulder. "Good luck, kiddo."

"Way to go, Josh," Dakota said, giving him the thumbs-up.

Everyone except a sulky-looking Brittany, who was picking at her nail polish, clapped as Josh walked up to the front and took his place on the chair. He opened the book to the page he'd bookmarked and slid the turquoise overlay into place. And then he looked up.

A sea of small faces looked back at him eagerly.

Wetting his lips, he imagined himself sitting on Mrs. Gordon's couch, with the clay shapes on the coffee table. Then he began.

"At that moment something hit the saucepan with

a loud ping, and ashes flew up out of the fire. A long arrow with a green feather stuck, quivering, among the embers."

Josh paused. The story was so real, it was as if he were right there, at the campsite on Wild Cat Island with John, Susan, Titty, and Roger. He could almost smell the smoke.

He continued reading.

"Roger grabbed at the arrow and pulled it out of the fire. Titty took it from him at once. 'It may be poisoned,' she said. 'Don't touch the point of it.'"

A gasp came from a boy on the floor. "Poisoned? Is the man on the houseboat really a pirate? What happens next?"

As Josh looked out, he saw the kids gazing at him, waiting for him to keep reading. Not a single one was sniggering or laughing at him. He caught Mrs. Gordon's eye and grinned. "You'll have to read the book to find out."

Acknowledgements

I owe thanks to a great number of people who helped me along the journey of writing this book. To my wonderful publisher, Diane Morriss, who said those magic words, "I want to publish your book," despite my thinking she was a telemarketer and ignoring her phone calls for more than a few days. To my super editor, Barbara Pulling, who asked all the right questions to get me thinking about the story in a whole new way. To Dawn Loewen, who not only did a fabulous job of copy editing, but also shared the story with Verna Miller, a retired special-education teacher, for extra input on the manuscript. To Frances Hunter for her beautiful design, and to the rest of the Sono Nis Press team for their encouragement and support. To Tammy Moore at the Victoria READ Society for sharing her methods for teaching reading to children with dyslexia (any mistakes are mine!). To Michael Storer, designer of the Goat Island Skiff, for inspiring and building a community of backyard boatbuilders all over the world. To Bronwyn and Helen for eagle-eyed proofreading. To Carol, Robin, and Sarah, writing instructors extraordinaire. To all my critique buddies online, including Carrie, Jamie, Judy, Julie, Wendy, and Marsha of Kidcrit. To my local writing friends Jo, Katharine, Lea, Nancy, Sue, and especially Kathy and Pauline for believing in the story and me even when I didn't. And not least, to my husband, Patrick, for patiently listening to the many rough drafts and offering insightful suggestions at just the right time. Thank you!

Resources

Victoria READ Society: www.readsociety.bc.ca
Michael Storer Boat Plans: www.storerboatplans.com

ABOUT THE AUTHOR

Jenny Watson grew up in small-town New Zealand, dreaming of big adventures in faraway places. When she was eighteen, she spent a year as an exchange student in Thailand, where she learned to speak a little Thai (*nit noi*) and to eat curry and sticky rice with her fingers. After returning to New Zealand to earn a master's degree in psychology, she moved to San Diego and trained to be a technical writer. Jenny, her husband, and their small but feisty parrot now make their home in Victoria, B.C. They grab every opportunity they can to go sailing with friends until they launch their very own plywood sailing dinghy.